Devil on Canyon Road

Also by James C. Wilson from Sunstone Press:

Hiking New Mexico's Chaco Canyon: The Trails, The Ruins, The History

New Mexico's Chaco Canyon, Photographing the Ancient City

Santa Fe, City of Refuge: An Improbable Memoir of the Counterculture

The Fernando Lopez Santa Fe Mystery Series:

Peyote Wolf
Smokescreen
Ghost Canyon
The Dead Go Fast
Painted Skull Ranch
Taos Gothic
Taos Vendetta

DEVIL ON CANYON ROAD

A FERNANDO LOPEZ SANTA FE MYSTERY

JAMES C. WILSON

SUNSTONE PRESS

SANTA FE

Sunstone books may be purchased for educational, business, or sales promotional use.
For information please write: Special Markets Department, Sunstone Press,
P.O. Box 2321, Santa Fe, New Mexico 87504-2321.
Printed on acid-free paper
∞
eBook 978-1-61139-715-4

Library of Congress Cataloging-in-Publication Data

Names: Wilson, James C., 1948- author. | Wilson, James C., 1948- Fernando
Lopez Santa Fe mystery.
Title: Devil on Canyon Road : a Fernando Lopez Santa Fe mystery / James C.
Wilson.
Description: Santa Fe : Sunstone Press, [2023] | Series: A Fernando Lopez
Santa Fe mystery | Summary: "The murder of a homeless man and reports of
a red-faced prowler seen on Canyon Road trigger rumors of the Devil
loose in Santa Fe, but Private Investigator Fernando Lopez discovers
more sinister threats from anti-immigrant politicians and the Sinaloa
Cartel from Mexico"-- Provided by publisher.
Identifiers: LCCN 2023019931 | ISBN 9781632935403 (paperback) | ISBN
9781611397154 (epub)
Subjects: LCSH: Lopez, Fernando (Fictitious character) |
Murder--Investigation--Fiction. | Santa Fe (N.M.)--Fiction. | LCGFT:
Detective and mystery fiction.
Classification: LCC PS3623.I58485 D48 | DDC 813.6--dc23/eng/20230509
LC record available at https://lccn.loc.gov/2023019931

WWW.SUNSTONEPRESS.COM
SUNSTONE PRESS / POST OFFICE BOX 2321 / SANTA FE, NM 87504-2321 /USA
(505) 988-4418

Dedicated to the international agencies, nonprofit organizations, and individuals who help immigrants find refuge and new lives.

"La plus belle des ruses du diable est de vous persuader qu'il n'existe pas."
—Charles Baudelaire, *Paris Spleen*

Under the Bridge

Mike Carter had lost all sense of time. It must be nearly Midnight, because most everyone had left El Farol except for the heavy drinkers. One of them, a big loud-mouthed guy wearing red Bermuda shorts, had treated him to a beer earlier, even if he'd had to drink it sitting outside on the front porch. Sonsabitches wouldn't let him drink in the bar because they thought he looked like a dirty bum, not a homeless guy down on his luck. He felt dizzy when he stood up, so he held on to the railing for a few seconds to get his balance. He couldn't remember the last time he'd eaten anything. Yesterday morning, maybe.

On the way down the porch steps he stumbled and fell forward on his hands and knees. He sat on the sidewalk for a few minutes, breathing deeply, trying to clear his head. The palms of his hands stung like hell from landing on the sidewalk. Finally he picked himself up and adjusted his backpack.

Shoulders slumped, he shuffled across Canyon Road into the parking lot, where something caught his eye: a flash of red in the trees beyond the lot. He thought it must be a taillight from down below on East Alameda Street. Somehow he had to get down to Alameda and then walk to the Delgado Street Bridge. His camp waited for him there under the protection of the bridge. He could sleep until morning and then go looking for food. The cooks at the Inn on the Alameda had been helping him recently, maybe they would give him some leftover breakfast. Might as well give it to him. They just threw it away anyway. What a country. Some people starve, while rich people stuff themselves and throw away what they can't eat.

Branches scratched his arms and face as he waded into the stand of trees, beyond which he came to a long yard that sloped down to the Santa Fe River. Ahead of him he saw huge dark shapes erected in the yard. It took him a few moments to realize he had entered a sculpture garden, with huge gargoyles and winged animals lurking in the shadows. He moved carefully among the ghoulish shapes, trying to be as quiet as possible. He didn't want to wake whoever owned the place and get shot just trying to walk to his damn camp.

Somewhere off to his left a dog barked loudly, giving him pause. All he needed now was a watchdog on the loose. He looked around hoping to find shelter in case the dog attacked. He spotted a flat bed truck parked at the end of the yard, probably for hauling around those big-ass sculptures. If the dog attacked, he could climb on the bed of the truck and hope it was too high for the dog to follow. If the dog did manage to jump up on the bed, he would kick the goddamned thing in the snout and send it flying, he would. He'd done it before.

Fortunately, the dog stopped barking. False alarm.

Quickening his pace, he headed down toward the dark riverbank under a moonless sky. From where he walked he could see the bridge about one hundred yards further along the river. A nearby streetlight bathed the bridge in a pale yellow light, which quickly dissolved in the surrounding darkness. He fought his way through the trees and brush along the riverbank, guided by the glow of the streetlight.

Closer to the bridge he thought he heard branches snapping behind him, but when he turned around he saw nothing but trees, jagged shadows in the murky night. Hurrying, he slipped on the riverbank and slid down to the water's edge. He picked himself up and staggered toward the bridge, desperate to reach camp before he lost what energy he had left. All he wanted to do now was crawl into his tattered sleeping bag and sleep. Tomorrow he would worry about food.

Finally he saw the bridge straight ahead, with its comforting dark space underneath where he'd pitched his camp against the concrete foundation. He stumbled the last few paces. He didn't care how much noise he made. When he reached the safety of the bridge he stopped and put his hands on his knees, trying to get his breath. Suddenly he heard the sound of footsteps approaching behind him.

He panicked, thinking it was the police. Or worse, a thief intent on robbing him and taking what little he had.

He balled his fists and spun around, gasping at what he saw: a bloated red face with huge pointed ears. He screamed, looking into the blood red eyes of an angry, distorted face. The lopsided face seemed to bleed, melting away like a face in a wax museum, oozing blood.

He closed his eyes as the first blow came, knocking him backwards. His eyes filled with tears from the pain. Before he could move a metal object slashed across his face and then his neck. He pitched forward feeling the warm wetness of his blood. Clutching his neck, he fell under the bridge into the darkness.

1

It started with a voice mail. Private Investigator Fernando Lopez walked into his office on Canyon Road and spotted the flashing light on his desk phone. He replaced the 'Closed' sign in his front window with the 'Open' sign and took a seat at his desk. His phone told him he had one message waiting. He hit the play button on his phone and listened to the caller mumbling something inaudible, followed by a series of noises that sounded like the caller had dropped the phone. Moments later a hoarse, scratchy voice croaked, "Uh...Lopez...I need your help. The Devil's after me! I saw him last night on Canyon Road. Big red face dripping blood... with flames coming out of him like fires from the pits of hell! Wait... what?" The line went dead and the message ended.

Fernando recognized the feeble voice of Wayne Fontenot, an eighty-year-old painter who lived in a run-down guest house further up Canyon Road. A drunk and ne'er-do-well, Wayne was one of a group of artists who met nearly every evening to drink at the El Farol Bar. Fernando thought it likely Wayne suffered from early stage dementia, but no one knew for sure if he'd been officially diagnosed. Wayne had a habit of leaving crazy messages on Fernando's answering machine. Just last week Wayne had called saying he'd seen the Governor posing nude on the Plaza. Turned out it was a troupe of cheerleaders from Santa Fe High celebrating the upcoming fall football season. The Governor was not present, and the cheerleaders in question were clothed, however scantily. On occasion Wayne had flashbacks, thinking he was living in a different time and place. With Wayne, you never knew what you were going to get. A real piece of work.

So Fernando did the same thing he did with each and every one of Wayne's messages: deleted it. One push of the delete button and the problem was solved. If the Devil had indeed appeared on Canyon Road, let somebody else deal with it. Religion or mythology, whatever you wanted to call it, was not his area. He was a secular private investigator living and operating in the material world.

Fernando leaned back in his chair, put his feet up on the desk, and opened his morning *Santa Fe Independent*. Since retiring last year as a Santa Fe Police Detective, he'd set up his shingle as a private investigator in a former garage his old friend Ruby Montez let him use and remodel. With new carpet and wood paneling, the place looked like a real office. He took his sweet time every day, showing up at his office about ten o'clock every morning and leaving by four. So far he'd averaged two or three clients a week, mostly related to missing family members: a husband who'd run off with his secretary to Los Angeles, or a daughter who'd run off with her boyfriend to Las Cruces or Austin. Fine with him. He enjoyed a lighter workload after thirty long years in the Santa Fe Police Department.

As noon approached Fernando started thinking about lunch. He decided to go next door to Ruby's gallery and ask if she wanted to go down the street to El Farol for lunch. He'd seen her Honda Accord next to the gallery when he pulled into the parking lot this morning. So he tossed the *Independent* in the wastebasket and walked to the door, intending to put his 'Closed' sign back in the window. Before he could change signs, he spotted none other than Wayne Fontenot hobbling down the gravel path to his office. His spirits sank. Now he would have to listen to Wayne's incoherent ramblings about the Devil or whatever else he had on his mind. So much for lunch.

Fernando watched the plump, hunch-backed artist poke at the gravel with his cane as if he were killing snakes. Wayne wore the same black suit he'd worn for at least the past ten years, topped off by a gray felt hat squashed down on his head. His long, unkempt white beard gave him the look of a demented Santa Claus.

Fernando bit the bullet and opened his door wide to allow for entry.

Wayne raised his cane and shook it at Fernando. "So...what are we gonna do about this situation?"

"What situation?" Fernando asked.

"The Fiend, you idiot," Wayne shot back, huffing and puffing. "Didn't you get my message? He walks among us!"

Fernando took Wayne inside and sat him down in the chair facing his desk so the old man could catch his breath. "Okay, why don't you tell me what happened. From the beginning."

Wayne nodded. "Well, when I left Claude's night before last I started walking home by myself. Dave Stein left earlier, so I was alone. Jimmy Mackey didn't even show up that night. I don't know what the hell happened to him. All I know's he shouldn't have married that Ruby Montez, what a fool he was. Everybody knows that woman is nothing but trouble. She almost called the cops on me for loitering the other day. Hell, I was just looking for Jimmy."

Fernando raised his hand. He couldn't listen to anymore. "Wayne, Jimmy's dead. He was murdered over a year ago in Taos. Don't you remember? You came to his memorial service at El Farol."

Wayne stared at Fernando, not comprehending. "Whatever you say, but let me finish my goddamn story, will you? You keep interrupting me. Like I said, I came outa Claude's and started walking back home when I saw a big red face in the trees. I mean big, with horns and everything. At first I thought it was Claude herself, you know how she dresses crazy like that sometimes, especially when she sings cabaret in the bar wearing those costumes."

Fernando went to raise his hand and then thought better of it. Why bother? Instead, he let Wayne drone on about Claude, who'd been dead since 1985. Wayne always confused El Farol with Claude's, a celebrated and deservedly famous bar on Canyon Road owned by Claude James, a New Yorker who happened to stop in Santa Fe on a Western jaunt and decided to stay. She opened Claude's in the mid fifties and ran it until the late seventies. A Santa Fe legend, Claude was both cabaret singer and bouncer in her bar, one of the first bars in Santa Fe to welcome people of all sexual preferences. Before terms like gender neutral and nonbinary became common parlance, Claude blazed the path, the real deal. Normally she dressed in men's clothes––shirt, slacks, and sport coat––but when she sang, accompanied by a pianist, she wore long elaborate gowns and dared anyone to make a comment. Few did.

Fernando remembered Claude only too well. He celebrated his twenty-first birthday at Claude's with several unruly friends, none of them able to hold their liquor. When they irritated Claude with their juvenile behavior she threw them out––threw them out physically. Starting with Fernando, she grabbed each one of them by the belt and drug him to the door, where she sent him on his way with a swift kick in the ass. As the saying goes, she didn't suffer fools lightly. She kicked them in the ass and sent them on their way.

"Are you listening to me?" Wayne asked, bringing Fernando back to the moment, out of his memories.

"Yes, Wayne, I'm listening," Fernando said, a slight exaggeration. "So tell me why you think this Devil, this Fiend with a red face, is after you?"

"Because last night he followed me home from the bar, that's why. I saw him in the trees again, and then when I got to my street, he followed me part way up the alley until I turned and shouted "Demon, be gone!""

Fernando laughed. "And that sent him running, did it?"

"Why are you laughing, Lopez? What's so funny about the Devil?"

Fernando shrugged. "Sorry. So what happened next? Did he leave?"

Wayne shook his head. "Not until I quoted the prayer to Saint Michael, the Archangel. I looked the Fiend in the eye and repeated the prayer. You know, 'blah blah blah, by the power of God, thrust into hell Satan, and all the evil spirits, who prowl about the world, seeking the ruin of souls.'"

Wayne's recall impressed Fernando.

"You know the prayer, you're a damned Catholic, right?"

"Lapsed Catholic," Fernando said. "Been a long time."

Wayne nodded.

"So describe this Fiend. You said he had a red face dripping blood and flames coming out of him?"

"Damned right," Wayne said. "His body was black as charcoal. And like I said, his face was blood red. Scared the hell out of me at first, until I remembered Michael. That sent him running back into the trees where he belongs, I guess."

"So he's gone, then," Fernando said, eager to end the conversation so he could go to lunch. "Why are you worried?"

Wayne stared at Fernando, as if not believing what he'd just heard. "Well, what's gonna happen when he attacks someone who isn't a Catholic...or doesn't know Michael's Prayer? You see the problem?"

Fernando sighed. "So what do you want me to do, Wayne?"

"Well...."

Fernando waited.

"Why don't you call one of the people you know down at the Independent," Wayne said. "You know, ask them to print a full-page warning about the Devil being on Canyon Road. Maybe they could include a copy of Michael's Prayer, so everybody in Santa Fe could memorize it and be prepared to fight off the demon."

"Okay, I'll do it. Anything else?" Fernando asked, checking his watch.

Wayne gave him the Evil Eye, not sure if Fernando was serious. Finally he tapped his cane on the floor and managed to get up out of the chair without falling. He waved goodbye with his cane and headed for the door.

Just before he reached the door, Wayne turned and said, "If you see Jimmy, tell him to stop by my studio."

2

Fernando watched Wayne hobble off toward Canyon Road. He noticed that Wayne walked like a penguin, bobbing from side to side while poking with his cane. He waited until Wayne disappeared from sight and then closed his office and walked over to Ruby's gallery, which she'd inherited from her ex-husband Jimmy Mackey after Jimmy was murdered in Taos last year.

He and Ruby went back a long way, even before he met and married his wife, Estelle. Always prickly, Ruby wore her bad attitude with pride. To her, it was a badge of honor. Her in-your-face personality put off many people but had made her a force in Santa Fe politics for over two decades. A potter by trade, Ruby had risen through the ranks of *La Raza* to become the most progressive member of City Council ever. Back in the 1990s she fought tooth and nail against all the greedy developers who wanted to turn downtown Santa Fe into one big shopping mall. She led rallies, marches, protests, sit-ins, and if you believed the rumors, a fire-bombing or two.

She lost, of course. The developers and the Sotheby's crowd turned Santa Fe into Disneyland Southwest. The tide of gentrification sweeping over Santa Fe during those years hollowed out the city. Gone were most of the people whose families had lived in Santa Fe for generations. Increasingly higher home values and property taxes priced out all who couldn't afford the million dollar homes. After two tumultuous terms on City Council lecturing, berating, cajoling, and threatening the other members, she said 'fuck it' and retired to the pottery co-op she owned and ran with a number of other potters, most of them women.

Still she refused to be silenced. She made it a point to attend most Council meetings and give the members a piece of her mind. Every one of them feared Ruby's tirades. Occasionally her anger would get the better of her language and she would be asked to leave. Once a few years back City Council banned her for a year, but her lawyer, Raoul Garcia, sued their asses and got her reinstated in her front row seat staring down the Council.

Over the years he and Ruby had always been friendly, probably because they felt the same way about gentrification and Santa Fe politics in general. That is, they usually ended up on the losing side.

Fernando walked into the gallery and spotted Ruby in what had been Jimmy's kitchen, now Ruby's office. She wore her work clothes, jeans and a blue cotton shirt with a red bandana around her dark hair. Even from afar Fernando spotted the flecks of potter's clay on her face and clothing. She looked like she'd just come from her pottery co-op in the Railyard District.

"Hey, Fernando, what's up?" she called out from her office.

"How about lunch at El Farol?" he asked, admiring both the ceramics displayed in cases and the colorful paintings of Jimmy's still hanging on the walls. A riot of color.

"No can do," Ruby said. "Carol got sick this morning, so I had to leave my wheel at the co-op and take over. Then I got caught up in the police crime scene on Delgado Street."

"What crime scene?" Fernando asked.

Ruby shrugged. "Looked like they found somebody dead under the Delgado Street Bridge near Alameda. They had a body on a stretcher and were loading it in an ambulance. Big traffic jam."

Fernando hesitated, thinking he may have to reconsider his plan for lunch.

"Yeah, I didn't even have time to change before I came in," Ruby said. "I look like shit."

Fernando laughed. "At our age, who cares?"

"Nobody. That's the God's truth," Ruby said. "Come on back. You can share the bag lunch I packed for the co-op."

Fernando walked into the office, where Ruby had kept the kitchen counter and two bar stools for coffee and lunches. She took paper plates out of a cupboard and then served salad fixings and half a sandwich on each of the two.

"There's beer and water in the fridge, help yourself," Ruby said.

Fernando grabbed a bottle of water out of the refrigerator and pulled up a stool.

"So what's new?" Ruby asked, picking at her salad. "I haven't seen you since last week."

Fernando told her about Wayne's visit and his claim that the Devil himself had appeared on Canyon Road and was stalking him.

Ruby looked up at him. "The Devil? As in Satan?"

Fernando nodded. "He says he saw the Devil outside El Farol. Twice, in fact, and the second time the Devil chased him all the way home. He described the Devil as having a big red face dripping blood and a black body, burned the color of charcoal."

Ruby stopped eating. "Thanks, that's real appetizing."

Fernando grinned. "He wants me to contact the *Independent* and ask them to print an ad warning people about the Devil on Canyon Road."

Now Ruby laughed. "Hah! It's no accident Wayne saw the Devil on his way out of El Farol, given the amount of booze he drinks every night. Maybe he looked in the mirror. The man's bat-shit crazy."

"I know. Every week he leaves at least one crazy message on my answering machine."

"He still thinks Jimmy is alive," Ruby said. "He comes in here all the time asking to see Jimmy. I kid you not."

"Even worse, he thinks Claude is still alive."

Ruby choked on her sandwich and had to take a drink of water. "Claude James?"

Fernando nodded.

"Jesus, she's been dead for forty years," Ruby said, then paused a moment before continuing. "Although rumor had it they had an affair back in the day. And I mean way back in the day."

"I thought Claude was a lesbian," Fernando said.

"Yeah, but Claude would swing however she wanted to swing, if you know what I mean. You monogamists wouldn't understand."

Fernando laughed at that, knowing Ruby had a long history of swinging both ways.

After lunch Fernando walked back to his office and checked his voice mail. No messages. So he decided to head down to the Delgado Street Bridge to check on the police action. See what that was all about.

He drove up Canyon Road and on around to East Alameda Street. He took Alameda down to Delgado Street and saw two police cruisers still parked on the sidewalk near the bridge. He found a parking meter just past the Paseo, where he usually parked when he came downtown. It was a short walk up Alameda to the Delgado Bridge over the Santa Fe River.

Manny Alvarez, Fernando's replacement as lead detective at the Santa Fe Police Department, sat at a picnic table alongside the river scribbling in a notebook. Another cop he didn't know, this one in uniform, paced back and forth under the bridge looking for evidence.

Manny looked up when he noticed Fernando approaching. "Hey, bro, see what you're missing."

"No, what happened?" Fernando asked the short, skinny man wearing jeans and an oversize sports coat.

"Just your ordinary corpse under the bridge," Manny said, joking. "He was homeless, camped along the river. A jogger reported him this morning after noticing the smell."

Manny joked a lot, which offended some people. Fernando had grown used to Manny's sense of humor, but not the Chief, who regularly reprimanded Manny for his smart-ass comments. Manny became lead detective by default when Fernando retired. The only other detective on the force was Armando, who was even younger and more inexperienced than Manny.

Fernando nodded. "What do you have so far?"

"Guy's name was Mike Carter, fifty seven years old and living under the bridge with nothing but a backpack," Manny said. "Looks like someone attacked him on his way back to his camp. He had a sleeping back and some personal belongings hidden in the bushes. Nothing of any value."

"How was he killed?"

"Sliced and diced, my friend," Manny said, with a smile. "His attacker slashed his face and his jugular. Even slashed his wrist. Almost like he was trying to drain the man's blood. Like a vampire, except no teeth marks on the neck."

Fernando frowned. He didn't like what he was hearing.

"That's not all. We had another similar case last week--a homeless guy camped out behind Fort Marcy Park," Manny added. "Same thing. Neck and wrists slashed, as if his blood was being drained."

"Anything else in common?" Fernando asked.

"Well, this will sound weird, but both men had traces of red paint on their wrists where they were grabbed or held down," Manny said. "Looks like we have a serial killer on our hands."

Red paint? Fernando mused, remembering Wayne's description of the face he saw in the woods. "Maybe Wayne wasn't as crazy as he thought.

3

After he left the Delgado Street Bridge Fernando drove back to his office and checked his answering machine. No messages. So he said the hell with it and headed home. He drove down to the Paseo and around to Acequia Madre Street. He and his wife Estelle had lived in their small adobe on Acequia Madre for over thirty years. Theirs was the last of the original small adobes on the street, tucked away among the million dollar mansions built or remodeled by the wealthy newcomers from New York and Los Angeles. He parked in the driveway, noticing Estelle's Camry in the garage. The open garage door meant Estelle had forgotten to close the door or would be going out again after dinner.

He climbed out of his Cherokee and walked across their patio to the kitchen door. He saw Estelle through the screen door making an early dinner. Estelle still looked youthful after forty years of marriage, with short gray hair and not a wrinkle on her face. Ironically their workloads had reversed after his retirement. He now had the easier schedule, setting his own hours and taking on whatever work he wanted. Estelle, on the other hand, worked long hours for the Saint Francis Immigrant Outreach Program, a religious nonprofit that provided goods and services for the ever-growing immigrant community in Santa Fe, a sanctuary city. The numbers of the people they served seem to grow monthly. Now the immigrants were coming from as far away as Afghanistan and the Ukraine.

"Grab some bowls, will you?" Estelle said when he walked into the kitchen. "I just made posole and a salad. I have to be at the church by six. We're delivering food tonight."

"Sure," he said, noticing that she was wearing her work clothes: jeans and a black cotton sweater.

He set the table while Estelle brought the food. Then he took a can of Modelo out of the refrigerator and popped the top. Usually he liked to drink a beer before dinner. Tonight would be rushed.

"So how was your day?" Estelle asked. "Any new clients?"

Over dinner Fernando told her about Wayne Fontenot's visit, how he claimed to have seen the Devil on Canyon Road and was convinced the Devil was after him. He repeated Wayne's description of the Fiend, not knowing how Estelle would react. Estelle had been a dedicated Catholic all her life. She attended mass virtually every Sunday and had worked for the parish in one capacity or another the entire time they had been married, most recently for the Immigrant Outreach Program.

Unlike Estelle, Fernando rarely attended mass. After thirty years of police work, he believed in a material world, cut and dried. He admired people who believed; he just couldn't.

Estelle looked at him thoughtfully and asked, "So how did Wayne fend off the Devil?"

Fernando laughed. "He said he shouted 'Demon be gone!' and recited the Prayer to Michael the Archangel."

"And do you believe his story?" Estelle asked.

"No, of course not," Fernando said. "He's a drunk and has some degree of dementia."

Estelle nodded. "But it worked, right?"

Fernando had no response to that, so he asked, "What about you? Where will you be distributing tonight?"

She sighed. "On the West side again. I'm a little worried about this new group in town, Take Back Our Streets. They might cause trouble. There's supposed to be a demonstration on the Plaza this evening."

"Never heard of them," Fernando said.

"Oh, you will," Estelle said. "They're running candidates for City Council this Fall. They blame immigrants and homeless people for the city's increase in crime. They want to send all immigrants back across the border and put all homeless people in camps."

"Camps? What kind of camps?"

"Yeah, you know, like internment or work camps, somewhere south of the city," Estelle said. "Maybe out toward La Bajada Hill."

Fernando shook his head. "Who are these people?"

"The same rich people who oppose the building of group homes or low income housing in their neighborhoods," Estelle said. "Anglos Mostly, but not all. From what I can tell, Rodger Barkley and Homer Tryzinski are the leaders. They're supposed to speak this evening on the Plaza."

As soon as they finished dinner Estelle grabbed a light jacket and took off in her Camry, leaving Fernando to do the dishes and put away the food. When finished, he brewed himself a cup of coffee and went out on the patio to brood about this Take Back Our Streets gang. He knew Barkley and Tryzinski from his days as a Santa Fe Police Detective. Never particularly cared for either of them, both wealthy newcomers to Santa Fe from the East Coast. Ironic that so many of the newcomers claimed to love Santa Fe and then proceeded to barricade themselves in million dollar houses and gated communities.

Fernando finished his coffee, enjoying the crisp late summer evening. The leaves were just starting to turn on the big cottonwoods along the acequia. The fresh alpine air invigorated him.

Feeling renewed, Fernando decided to check out the protest on the Plaza. He locked the house and drove his Cherokee downtown, parking as he always did on Alameda Street. He realized he was becoming more obsessive-compulsive as he aged, but so what. It gave him comfort even if some of his repetition compulsions annoyed Estelle.

He walked up Old Santa Fe Trail past the La Fonda Hotel. As he approached San Francisco Street he saw a small crowd gathered near the bandstand on the Plaza, directly across the street from the Palace of the Governors. The gathering was smaller than he expected. Everyone these days seemed to love rabble-rousers, so he expected a larger crowd of sympathizers. He walked into the Plaza, frowning at the makeshift wooden structure that had replaced the obelisk that had stood on the Plaza for over a hundred years. The Soldiers' Monument had fallen victim to yet another group of anti-whatever protesters who had torn it down last year in a riot of self-righteousness. Now, apparently, the immigrant and homeless communities would be the target.

Fernando spotted Sergeant Antonio Blake standing off to the side, keeping an eye on the proceedings. At six feet eight inches tall and two hundred and eighty pounds, Antonio was known as the enforcer. Few people dared to cross him. Those who did paid a dear price.

"What's up, Antonio?" Fernando asked.

"Just watching these clowns," Antonio said. "More troublemakers. That's all we need in this town."

Fernando noticed more people arriving as they spoke. Quickly the crowd grew to thirty or forty onlookers jostling for position around the bandstand. Some of them wore concealed carry holsters. Not a good sign.

The first person to speak was Rodger Barkley, a retired District Attorney who looked like he spent most of his time in the fitness club and tanning salon. Tall and slender with wavy gray hair, Barkley wore slacks and a white dress shirt open at the collar. He stepped forward holding a bullhorn in his right hand and a whisk broom in his left hand. He waved the whisk broom in front of him and shouted, "It's time to clean up our city, folks. Time to sweep up the trash and haul it out of town. I'm not just talking about the litter and the garbage, I'm talking about the people who leave it on our streets and in our parks. You can't walk in Fort Marcy Park or along the Santa Fe River without seeing the garbage and the needles and the human excrement that's been left behind by the outside scum who pollute our streets. I'm talking about the homeless population that you see everywhere downtown begging for money and harassing the good citizens of Santa Fe. And I'm talking about the increasing horde of immigrants the Mayor and City Council have foolishly allowed to enter what they're calling a 'sanctuary city.'"

The crowd cheered. Some of them raised their fists in the air to show support.

"Well, where's our sanctuary?" Barkley shouted. "Where's our sanctuary from the scum of the earth that pollute our city streets and parks? Tell me that?"

While the crowd roared, Homer Tryzinski stepped forward and took the bullhorn from Barkley. A short, pugnacious man with a crew cut, Tryzinski was a businessman who owned a well-known restaurant in Santa Fe. He wore jeans and a Hawaiian shirt sprinkled with pineapples. He shuffled his feet and pumped his arms, as if he were attempting to shadow box. A real clown, as Antonio had said.

"I'll tell you how we take back our streets," he barked into the bullhorn, picking up where Barkley left off. "You vote for Rodger Barkley and Homer Tryzinski for City Council. We'll clean up our streets and parks and send the refuse packing. I'm talking about the homeless and the immigrants who are polluting our city and overwhelming our city services. Vote Barkley and Tryzinski!"

As Tryzinski spoke, an armada of honking vehicles roared down Washington Avenue to the corner of the Plaza, where they turned left on East Palace Avenue. All of the vehicles were flying both the Stars and Stripes and the New Mexico state flag. Not redneck pickups, these were Range Rovers, Escalades, Mercedes and Lexus SUVs, belonging to Santa Fe's upper crust.

Fernando watched the armada honk its way up Palace Avenue toward the Paseo, wondering just what all these people were willing to do in order to 'take back' the streets of Santa Fe.

4

Fernando awoke to find the other side of the bed empty. Estelle had already started her day. He'd not had a chance to talk to her last night because she came home after he'd gone to bed. He wanted to catch her before she left for work, hoping that nothing untoward had happened last night at the clothing distribution. So he jumped out of bed, dressed quickly in last night's clothes, and hurried to the kitchen. Estelle stood at the stove scrambling eggs.

"Scrambled eggs with green chile and toast for breakfast," she said, already dressed for work. "Coffee's on the counter."

Fernando helped himself to a cup of coffee and sat at the kitchen table. "Are you okay? Did everything go as planned last night?"

Estelle shook her head. "No, it was a disaster. We met at the San Isidro Church on Agua Fria to sort the clothing. We'd just started going through the boxes when a group of young hooligans drove up in a van, about six of them. They ran through the parking lot where we were loading and kicked over the boxes and scattered the clothing all over the churchyard. We tried to stop them, but what could we do, a bunch of old ladies? It took forever to gather and sort all the clothing. Some of the clothes were dirty or damaged so we couldn't use them."

Fernando cursed. "Did they hurt anyone?"

"No, they just ransacked the supplies we'd gathered and then drove off," Estelle said.

"Do you know who these punks were?" Fernando asked.

"No, but we heard them talking," Estelle said. "I think they were paid to do this by the Take Back Our Streets people. The group doesn't want any goods or services to go to immigrants or homeless people. They just want those people out of the city."

"Why don't you ask the police for protection?" Fernando asked.

"We did. The Chief is sending an officer to provide security while we finish the job today. Today we're going to try again to distribute the clothing. We didn't have time last night after we picked up everything."

After breakfast Estelle left for San Isidro Church, while Fernando took his time. He showered and changed clothes, planning his day. He decided to call his long-time friend Fidel Rodriguez, a senior reporter at the *Independent*, Santa Fe's daily newspaper. Fidel might have more information on the Take Back Our Streets movement. So he called Fidel's cell phone number.

Fidel answered immediately, as he always did. "Fernando, what's up?"

"Hey, Fidel," Fernando said. "I need some information on this Take Back Our Streets group. Are you occupied? Can I stop by the news room for a chat?"

There was a pause at the other end of the line. Finally Fidel responded. "I think it's better if we meet somewhere else. I'll explain later."

"How about the coffee shop on Marcy?" Fernando asked.

"Too close. How about the Starbucks on the Plaza in half an hour?"

"I'll be there."

After he clicked off, Fernando began to wonder why Fidel couldn't talk in the newsroom, and why he preferred a coffee shop some distance from Marcy Street, where the *Independent* offices were located.

A few minutes later he drove down to Alameda Street and parked near the Saint Francis Cathedral. He wasted a few minutes in the La Fonda newsstand and then walked down San Francisco Street to the Starbucks. Fidel was already standing in line wearing what Fidel called his 'reporter's uniform': slacks, blue dress shirt, and paisley necktie. Only part of his wardrobe missing was the brown corduroy sports coat he wore in cold weather. Fernando joined him.

"Why the secrecy?" Fernando asked.

Fidel shook his head. "I'll tell you outside."

They both ordered coffee and took their paper cups outside to the Plaza. Fernando followed Fidel to an empty bench overlooking the bandstand and took a seat on the bench.

"Thing is," Fidel began, "I can't really talk about this in the newsroom. It's like everything else these days: political. How the newspaper staff feels about Take Back Our Streets falls along party lines. Righties love the group and think it's long overdue; Lefties hate it and think it's a violation of every moral principle, secular or religious. It's as if they were talking about Trump. There's no middle ground."

"Shocks me you have Righties in the newsroom," Fernando said.

"Hah! You'd be surprised."

"Well, what do you think?"

"I think they're a bunch of thugs," Fidel said. "A bunch of thugs who use the law and order issue to violate the civil rights of everyone they attack."

Fernando nodded, agreeing with everything he'd just heard. "So what's the scoop on the two homeless men murdered? Are they in any way connected to this group?"

"That's the question," Fidel said. "I don't know. What I do know is that tomorrow the paper's running a story about the 'vampire killer.' That's right, vampire, because Forensics has determined that both victims had lost about sixty percent of their blood by the time they died."

"Your editors want to sensationalize the story rather than pursue the connection between the murders and the Take Back Our Streets group," Fernando said.

"Exactly. Because the Take Back Our Streets group includes some very powerful people," Fidel said. "In fact, I think the Mayor sympathizes with them."

Fernando nodded. "What else did Forensics say about the two murders?"

Fidel sighed. "That both of them were slashed multiple times. Their throats, even their wrists. The murderer knew what he was doing, where to get blood quickly out of the body. And the victims were loners, they had no way to get help."

Fernando considered what he'd just heard.

"So why are you interested in all this?" Fidel asked. "Are you on a case?"

"Not exactly," Fernando said, and told Fidel about Wayne Fontenot's visit and his far-fetched story about seeing the Devil on Canyon Road, including Wayne's graphic description of the Devil.

Fidel stared at Fernando. "And you believe all this?"

Fernando shook his head. "No, but I'd like to know who--or what-- is preying on these homeless men."

"Vampires and the Devil," Fidel said. "Could it get any worse?"

5

After leaving Fidel, Fernando drove down Agua Fria Street to the San Isidro Church. He found the parking lot deserted. Estelle and the other workers from the Outreach program had already left to distribute the clothing they'd collected. The police officer providing security had left also, either returning to the station or following the Outreach workers.

So Fernando turned around in the empty parking lot and drove back downtown, taking the Paseo around to Canyon Road. He intended to spend the rest of the day in his office, just another normal day on Canyon Road. But he changed his mind as soon as he saw his office, realizing this wasn't just another normal day. Instead he kept on going up Canyon Road looking for the alley that would take him to Wayne Fontenot's guesthouse. He'd been there once, long time ago, when he came to check on reported gunshots and found a dead body at the edge of the foothills behind Wayne's adobe. Turned out to be another artist, a glass blower, down on his luck. Coroner ruled it a suicide.

About a half mile up Canyon Road Fernando spotted what looked like the alley he remembered, with a rustic wooden fence on one side and a bright blue adobe on the other. He slowed down and turned into the dirt alley, past a row of rusted garbage cans and into a gradual curve that took him up a slight hill to Wayne's dilapidated guesthouse, a washed-out pink adobe with a tin roof and a scattering of cast-off furniture and discarded art supplies littering the dirt yard. Looked like Wayne used his front yard as his personal landfill.

If he recalled correctly, always a big if, the original owner of the property was also an artist, another painter. Not having any family, the owner left both the main house and the guesthouse to Wayne. Wayne stayed in the guesthouse and let the larger adobe crumble and become rat-infested until the city condemned the structure as a public nuisance and tore it down. Fernando couldn't remember the dates. Must have been in the 1990s when Wayne inherited the property.

When Fernando pulled up in front of the faded pink adobe, he noticed its front door was wide open. Not a good sign. He scooted out of the Cherokee and walked into the yard, past a tangle of broken wooden easels and sawhorses and several piles of garbage rotting in the sun. Large chunks of the pink stucco on the front of the guesthouse had cracked and fallen off, revealing the chicken wire underneath. The two windows in front were so dirty they looked black. It was hard to imagine any light getting through glass that dirty, which struck Fernando as odd. Didn't painters prize natural light to paint? Maybe that was why the front door was wide open.

"Wayne?" Fernando said, not bothering to knock. He heard music playing inside, so he stepped into a dark, dusty, crowded room that stank faintly of garbage and something rotting.

Through the gloom of the poorly lit room he saw dozens of painted canvasses stacked against the walls. An unfinished painting of dark adobes under a full moon stood propped up on one easel. Two ancient stuffed chairs crowded a small wooden table in the back of the room. On the table a radio broadcasted what sounded like Native American chants, the kind of music radio station KUNM played periodically throughout the day. Given the radio, it seemed logical to assume Wayne was somewhere hereabouts or would be returning soon.

"Wayne?" he said.

Again there was no reply.

Fernando moved into the primitive kitchen, which had a bulky refrigerator that must have been decades old. On its side hung an aged yellow flyer announcing "Claude's, the 'Rendezvous' of Santa Fe...Dining & Dancing with a French Accent." Since Claude's had closed in the 1970s, the flyer had to be nearly fifty years old. Next to the refrigerator a faded linoleum countertop was covered with dirty dishes. Instead of a water faucet the kitchen had a pump handle hanging over a small sink stained black by years of use. Garbage everywhere.

Reeling, he moved back into the main room, noticing a stack of tattered magazines on the floor. He peeked into the bedroom, a tiny room no bigger than a closet with an unmade single bed shoved under a black window. He avoided the bathroom altogether. He wondered if the bathroom had running water but didn't bother to check. Instead, he moved over to the easel and glanced again at the unfinished painting. Dark, very dark. So he took out his cell phone and clicked on the flashlight app. What he saw reminded him of Andrew Dasburg's paintings of Taos adobes set against a blue sky. Except Wayne's adobes were dark and set against a gray ominous sky under the glow of a full moon. The full moon provided just enough light to illuminate a red face peering out of a stand of aspen trees off to the side of the adobes. A red face rimmed by horns or gigantic ears, he couldn't tell which. Not only that, but the red face was blurred by thick gobs of paint, as if the face were melting down the canvas. It was identical to Wayne's description of the red face he's seen in the trees across from El Farol. The face of the Devil.

Next Fernando turned his light on a table beside the easel. He saw a scattering of painting supplies spread out on the table, including tubes of oil and acrylic paints, brushes and cleaning solvents, old paint-crusted palettes, and something else. He did a double-take and saw the same thing: a test tube among the tubes of paint. He took a handkerchief out of his back pocket and picked up the test tube. It had a trace of a dried substance inside, a reddish brown liquid. Looked like dried blood, but why would Wayne have a test tube filled with blood? It made no sense whatsoever. Typical of Wayne.

He put the test tube back where he found it and walked outside where the late summer sun scalded the foothills and shimmered the air in front of him. Uncertain of his next move, he circled the small adobe looking for signs of a struggle, anything that would explain Wayne's absence. It was as though Wayne had walked away leaving his radio on and his front door wide open. Why?

In a stand of piñon and juniper trees behind the house he found a fire pit and a wooden picnic table gray with age, along with a creaky wooden bench. No sign anyone had used the fire pit recently. Beyond the trees several footpaths took off in different directions. One path led to an old Forest Service building about a mile above Wayne's house. The other paths led to the foothills and then up into the Sangre de Cristo Mountains.

Giving up, Fernando retraced his steps to Wayne's house. He went inside and turned off the radio. The least he could do. Then he locked the front door and closed it behind him, hoping Wayne had taken his key with him, wherever he'd gone. He sat in the Cherokee for a few moments considering what to do next. The only people who might know Wayne's whereabouts were his drinking buddies at El Farol, namely Dave Stein and Blaine Rogers, both of whom would be at El Farol come Happy Hour, which was just about to start.

Time to get happy.

6

Fernando drove back to his office and checked his messages. Still nothing. He waited until five o'clock to give the Canyon Road artists time to wet their whistles and loosen their tongues. At five exactly he walked down Canyon Road to El Farol, one of the many historic buildings in Santa Fe. The restaurant/bar dated from 1835 and was still going strong, hosting a variety of flamenco and other musical events. It was a great place to drink or eat, as everyone on Canyon Road could testify, especially the artistic types who usually skipped the eating.

As he approached the long porch in front he saw several people walking across Canyon Road from the parking lot. He followed them, stepping up on the porch where two couples were already sitting at the outdoor tables. A string of lights and red chile ristras hung from the ceiling of the porch, its beams and railings and windows painted a chocolate brown color that contrasted with the tan stucco on the adobe. After a recent remodel, the place looked like a million bucks.

Fernando walked into the noisy bar, already crowded with celebrants. Most everyone who came to El Farol was a regular, which was why the artists on Canyon Road loved it. He spotted Ruby back in the restaurant part of El Farol, sitting at a table in front of a flashy colored mural of musicians and flamenco dancers. Ruby sat next to Dave Stein, a wizened little man with olive skin that glowed and wisps of gray hair sticking up from various parts of his skull and out of his ears. Like Wayne, Dave was in his eighties and almost as forgetful. And like Wayne, Dave wore the same suit—in his case blue—that he'd worn for decades.

Fernando looked around but Wayne was nowhere to be seen. Unusual, very unusual.

"Fernando, come join us," Ruby called from across the room.

Fernando bought a Modelo draft at the bar and then walked over to the table and pulled up a chair. Ruby looked her gallery-owner finest today, with a low-cut silk blouse the color of wine and black slacks. "You look gorgeous, Ruby," he said.

"Hah! That's what they all say when they wanna get in my pants," Ruby shot back. "I'm not looking for husband number three, not even you, Fernando. Two husbands were two husbands too many."

He laughed. "Where's Wayne?"

Dave shrugged. Dave had a habit of looking like he was asleep until he moved or said something. Even then, when speaking, he talked with his mouth shut, like a ventriloquist without a dummy. Dave was ventriloquist and dummy both. "Bloodsuckers got him."

"Oh, don't listen to Dave, he was drunk when he got here," Ruby said, giving Dave a dirty look.

Just then Blaine Rogers burst into El Farol. "God-DAMN I need a drink," he said, a big, belligerent lout with a beer belly wearing red Bermuda shorts and a khaki fishing vest over a white T-shirt. Blaine always looked unkempt and a bit deranged, with long raven-black hair falling into his eyes and a voice that was several decibels too loud. The owner of Picasso and Co. Gallery, Blaine had for years sold the paintings of Ruby's dead ex-husband Jimmy Mackey and tried to sell the paintings of Wayne and Dave, even though neither of them produced anything tourists would be interested in buying. Blaine hadn't sold anything of theirs in years and only humored them by taking one or two of their paintings at a time.

Blaine swaggered over to the table and pulled up a chair. "Blaine's here, never fear. Let the party begin."

Ruby rolled her eyes. "Damn, Blaine, you get more full of yourself every time I see you."

"Yes, ma'am, I'm feeling good today," Blaine said. "I sold another of Jimmy's paintings today for a cool ten grand. I tell you, the best thing old Jimmy did was to go get himself murdered. We're cleaning up."

"So where's my cut? I was married to that lame-ass for almost a year. I want my eighty percent."

"Check's in the mail."

Just then Joanne, the server, brought Blaine his usual tequila shooter and a Dos Equis draft. "Thanks, darlin'. What time did you say your shift ended?"

Joanne laughed. "I didn't. It's just wishful thinking on your part."

"That's me, the year of wishful thinking," Blaine said. "Isn't there a book by that name?"

"Year of Magical Thinking," Ruby corrected Blaine. "I read it after

Jimmy died. It helped me get over the bastard."

Blaine shot back his tequila and drank down a third of his beer.

Fernando took a sip of his beer and then asked again, "So where's Wayne? I went to his house looking for him today. The door was wide open, and the radio was playing inside, but there was no sign of Wayne. Looked like he'd just walked out the door and disappeared."

Ruby shook her head. "I have no idea. He does this every once in a while. He'll go on a bender or get involved in a painting, forget to eat, that sort of thing. It's not that unusual for Wayne."

"That's my guess," Blaine said, agreeing with Ruby. "In fact, I think he could be working with a couple of new painters who just moved here from L. A. They rented that old Forest Service building behind Wayne's house, way up in the foothills. They came to my gallery the other day and showed me some of their work. I took two of their paintings. If they sell, I might give them a show."

"Bloodsuckers," Dave repeated.

Everyone looked at Dave.

"So who are these two interlopers from L.A.?" Ruby asked.

Blaine shrugged. "Hell if I know. Man and woman. Hipsters."

"Are they married?" Ruby asked.

"Jesus Christ! What am I, your social register?" Blaine boomed. "I have no idea and no interest in finding out. I don't give two shits about marriage—you should know that, Ruby."

Ruby laughed. "Yeah, I know you're not exactly the marrying type. No one would have you anyway, you bastard."

Blaine shot up from his chair and waved at the bartender. "Where's Joanne? I need another drink!"

Fernando continued to sip his Modelo, ignoring Ruby and Blaine and their endless bickering. He wondered: what exactly is a hipster. He couldn't get the word out of his mind. After another beer, he forgot about the word. And Wayne.

7

Fernando regretted ordering a second Modelo as he left El Farol, tired of listening to Ruby and Blaine argue. They sounded like an old married couple, like Ruby and her ex-husband Jimmy Mackey had sounded when their marriage was on the rocks, about a week after they tied the knot. He thanked his lucky stars that he and Estelle had avoided all that. They might not be as close as they once were, but at least they didn't bicker endlessly.

He walked across the street to his Cherokee under a darkening sky turning crimson in the west. He was about to drive off when his cell phone rang. He recognized the voice immediately.

"First ring, that's not bad for a retiree," Manny said, a real smart-ass. "I hate to bother you old timers but...."

Fernando put down the phone and let Manny drone on for a few seconds and then said, "So what's up, Manny, I'm a busy man."

"Yeah?" Manny asked. "Well, I have a situation out here at Marcy Park that you might be interested in, given what we talked about the other day––the homeless murders."

"I'm listening," Fernando said.

"Seems a bunch of hooligans raided the homeless camp here earlier this evening," Manny said. "They came through with baseball bats and busted up the camp, knocked over tents and chairs and clobbered whoever they could catch. Couple of homeless guys fought back. You remember Old Bill? Well, he grabbed a piece of iron used to tend the campfire and smacked one of the thugs over the head. Knocked him unconscious. We're waiting for the ambulance now. He's just starting to come around. I thought you might want to have a word with him before they haul him off to the Emergency Room."

"Have a word with him?" Fernando asked.

Manny laughed. "Yeah, because someone's paying these young punks to do this, right? And I think we both know that someone is connected to the Take Back Our Streets group."

"I'll be right there," Fernando said. "Hold him until I get there."

"Don't worry. He's in no condition to go anywhere except the Emergency Room," Manny said.

Fernando didn't waste any time. He drove down to the Paseo and around to Bishop's Lodge Road. Within minutes he turned onto the road leading to the Arroyo Barranca Trail. He saw the ambulance and two police cars up ahead. Manny stood behind the ambulance talking to Old Bill, a homeless man who had lived in and around Santa Fe for many years. No one knew his last name, so they all called him Old Bill because of his age. Farther back another cop helped several other homeless people collect their belongings and set up their tents again near the arroyo in the rear of the park. The tents looked damaged, lop-sided, thanks to the punks and their baseball bats.

Fernando pulled up alongside the ambulance and climbed out of his Cherokee.

"You remember Bill," Manny said to Fernando.

"Of course. Howdy, Bill," Fernando said.

Old Bill gave Fernando a mock salute. A nearly toothless old man who sometimes panhandled on the Plaza, Bill wore a stocking cap and an olive colored army jacket. As always, two strands of Mardi Gras beads hung from his neck, as though he was still partying from his last Mardi Gras. Over the years Bill had been able to provide information to Fernando and the Santa Fe Police on certain criminal cases because of his knowledge of street life. Old Bill claimed to know everything that went on in the streets.

"So these guys tried to destroy your camp?" Fernando asked.

"Hell yes they did," Old Bill snapped, offended. He motioned toward the injured man in the ambulance. "This sonofabitch knocked over my tent and hit me in the arm with a baseball bat. You should see the bruise. While he kicked over the rest of my stuff I grabbed the poker from the campfire and bashed him over the head. I'm sorry I didn't kill him!"

Fernando shook his head. "No, it's better you didn't."

"Next time them young punks come around I'll get my friends from the camp across the arroyo and we'll kick their asses," Old Bill said. "Teach them a lesson."

"How many of them were there?" Fernando asked.

"Four of the sonsabitches, but the driver just stayed in the car, a real chickenshit," Old Bill said. With that, Old Bill wandered over to help his fellow travelers restore their camp.

Manny shrugged. "Same Old Bill." He turned to the ambulance and said, "Here's the one they left behind. He was talking some earlier, but it looks like he's passed out again."

Fernando glanced at the young man lying on a stretcher: short, dark hair, dark skin, maybe early to mid twenties. Dressed all in black, the punk looked like he was out cold. A sizable pool of blood had formed under the guy's head.

"Looks like he needs to get to the ER fast," Fernando said.

"He's on his way, but I wanted you to see him first. And to see this," Manny said, showing Fernando a plastic evidence bag with a crisp hundred dollar bill inside. "This was the only thing in the guy's pockets. No identification of any kind. We have no idea who the guy is or what he was doing here, other than kicking hell out of the camp in exchange for a hundred dollar bill."

Fernando took a closer look. The punk's hands were as rough as sandpaper, his nails black with dirt. His unshaven face was sunburned with a thin white scar on his forehead and a longer scar on his left cheek. To Fernando he looked like a common day laborer, probably an illegal immigrant.

"So we need to find out who's paying these punks," Manny said.

Fernando nodded. "And you blame Take Back Our Streets."

Manny laughed. "Who else would be behind something like this? Just look who's involved. Sleazy Rodger Barkley, who had to resign as assistant district attorney because of accusations of money laundering. And Homer Tryzinski, who's about as subtle as a Mack truck. He looks more like a saloon bouncer than a businessman."

"I don't know, Manny," Fernando said. "These people have a lot to lose. It's hard for me to imagine they would do something like this."

"Yeah? Then who?"

Manny's question hung in the air.

Fernando shrugged. "I have no idea. There's a lot of anti-immigration talk these days, so who knows. You hear it at the City Council meeting every month. From councilmembers as well as members of the community who come to speak at the meetings. Some of them are just as bad as the right-wing councilmembers. Could be just a bunch of hooligans who want to take matters into their own hands."

"I suppose, but then who's passing out hundred dollar bills? Tell me that."

Fernando nodded. "At any rate, it's your call. Your case."

Manny gave him a strange look. "By the way, why are you so interested in this case anyway?"

"Let's just say I have a client who's concerned with all this," Fernando said, stretching the truth a bit. Could he claim Wayne Fontenot as a client? Even if he did, he wasn't about to broadcast Wayne's story of seeing the Devil on Canyon Road. No one would believe that nonsense. Especially coming from notoriously unreliable Wayne.

Now Manny was interested. "Really? Was your client attacked?"

Fernando shook his head. "No, but he was threatened on his way home this week."

Manny nodded. "Vampires and vigilantes. What's next?"

Biting his tongue, Fernando watched the ambulance drive off headed to Christus Saint Vincent Hospital.

Vampires and vigilantes were enough. He didn't want to add the Devil.

8

Next morning Fernando drove down to his office on Canyon Road at the usual hour. When he pulled into the parking lot, he saw someone lying flat on the bench near Essentia, the sex shop next door. It didn't look like Paul Bryan, who owned Essentia with his wife June. He climbed out of his Cherokee and walked across the parking lot to get a closer look. He recognized the suit as he came closer. None other than Wayne Fontenot, either sleeping or dead on the bench. His black suit was rumpled and dirty, with splotches of paint on the sleeves. His long white beard was dirty and matted with pieces of food.

Paul watched Fernando approach from his front porch. "Can you get that derelict off my bench? He's driving my customers away," he said, throwing up his arms.

"Hold on, I'm coming," Fernando said.

Fernando walked to the bench and pressed down on Wayne's shoulder. The old man failed to respond, so Fernando grabbed the shoulder and shook it roughly. "Wayne...are you dead?"

Wayne sputtered awake. "What? Dead? Hell, no. I've been waiting for you since eight o'clock this morning."

"Where have you been?" Fernando responded. "I stopped by your house yesterday looking for you. The door was wide open and the radio was playing inside, but no one was there."

Wayne sat up on the bench and looked around, as though checking to see if anyone was watching. "That's what I'm trying to tell you. Why I'm here."

Fernando frowned. "Okay, let's go in my office. We'll have more privacy, if that's what you want."

Wayne nodded and followed Fernando across the parking lot, hobbling along behind him.

Fernando unlocked the door and held it open for the old man.

Wheezing, Wayne hobbled to the chair and sat down across from the desk. He fought to catch his breath.

"You okay?" Fernando asked.

Wayne nodded. "Can't breathe...."

Fernando picked up the phone. "You want me to call nine one one?"

Wayne grabbed Fernando's arm, shaking his head. "No!"

Fernando put down the phone. "What's going on, Wayne? Why are you here?"

"I saw him again," Wayne wheezed.

"Saw who?"

"The Devil!" Wayne said. "What I'm trying to tell you."

Fernando sighed. He sat down at his desk and waited, staring at Wayne. The old man looked like the face of death: dirty, unkempt, his pasty white face a maze of wrinkles and sunspots ringed by a tangle of white hair.

Wayne spoke in short bursts of words, followed by desperate gasps for air. "Thing is...why I wasn't home...saw him again...followed him... locked me in a shed...tortured me."

"Who? Who tortured you?" Fernando asked, noticing the bandages on Wayne's fingers.

Unable to answer, Wayne suddenly slumped over in his chair while clutching his chest.

Fernando rushed around the desk. He grabbed the old man so he wouldn't fall out of the chair and felt for a pulse. Nothing at first, but then he felt what he thought was a weak pulse in Wayne's neck. He reached for the phone and dialed nine one one and asked for an ambulance immediately. Then he lifted Wayne out of the chair and gently laid him on the carpet. While waiting for the ambulance he did chest compressions, pushing with both hands on the dirty black suit coat in an effort to get the heart pumping again.

When he heard a siren coming up Canyon Road he ran outside and flagged the ambulance, which turned sharply into the parking lot. Two medics jumped out of the ambulance and followed him into the office. They dropped their bags on the carpet and went to work on Wayne. The older of the two medics began chest compressions, while the younger checked for pulse and blood pressure. Fernando didn't know either of them but was impressed by their speed and professionalism.

"What happened?" the older medic asked, a tall, lanky man with gray hair cut short.

"Looked like a heart attack," Fernando said. "He grabbed his chest and slumped forward. His name's Wayne Fontenot. He's a local artist who lives up the street. He has some form of mild dementia, maybe Alzheimer's, I'm not sure."

While they talked, the younger medic readied a needle and injected something in Wayne's arm, epinephrine most likely.

A few seconds later Wayne moved ever so slightly.

The older medic bent down to examine Wayne's bandaged hands. "What's this? Why the bandages?"

Fernando shook his head. "He said he was tortured."

Both medics looked at Fernando, who said, "That's all I know. What he said."

"It ain't every day you hear someone say they've been tortured," the old medic said.

With that, the young medic went out to the ambulance and returned with a stretcher. The two medics moved Wayne onto the stretcher and carried him to the ambulance.

The older medic came back for a moment. "You want to come with us to provide information?"

Fernando shook his head. "No, you'll find all the information you need in his wallet. I'm sure he's on Medicare or Medicaid, if you're worried about insurance."

The older medic looked offended. "I'm not worried about insurance. The hospital might be, but personally I don't give a damn." He closed the door and walked outside.

Shaken by the episode, Fernando sat at his desk and considered. Once again he had no idea how much credibility, if any, to assign to what Wayne said. If he understood correctly, Wayne claimed to have seen and pursued the Devil, only to be captured by the Fiend and locked in a shed where he was tortured. The bandages on his fingers provided some corroboration, however tenuous. Fact was, Wayne could have injured his hands a hundred different ways, most of them self-inflicted.

The more he thought about it, the sorrier he was for not accompanying Wayne to the hospital. He needed more information about what happened. He could only get that information from Wayne--a coherent Wayne.

So, reluctantly, Fernando locked up the office and climbed into his Cherokee. He took his time driving to Christus Saint Vincent Hospital on Saint Michael's Drive, wanting to give the Emergency Room nurses time enough to get Wayne situated in a room.

He found a space in the crowded Emergency Room parking lot and walked into the hospital. He introduced himself at the front counter, saying he was with Wayne Fontenot, the old timer who just came in by ambulance.

The woman behind the counter ignored him, busy with paperwork of some sort. Finally she looked up and asked, "Who are you with?"

"Wayne Fontenot," Fernando repeated. "Just came in on the ambulance."

The woman looked at him, a youngish, heavy-set woman with a round moon face and dark hair cut short. "Well, if he just came in, then he's being stabilized. Visitors will have to wait. Take a seat." She pointed to the already crowded waiting room, filled with crying kids and injured adults, some coughing and spewing into the air.

"Thanks," Fernando said and looked for a seat as far away from everyone as possible. He wasn't exactly a germaphobe, but the sight of all these sick people crammed into such a small space was worrisome.

He grabbed a free chair and dragged it into the hallway, ignoring the dirty looks he received from both staff and patients.

Nearly an hour later a young nurse came down the hallway and stopped. "Are you with Mr. Fontenot?"

"Yes, can I see him now," Fernando asked.

"Follow me," she said, a petite blonde dressed in blue with a stethoscope around her neck.

The nurse led Fernando down the hallway and into an open area surrounded by individual rooms for patients. He found Wayne in the first room. The old man lay on the bed wearing a hospital gown, his face as white as death but clean, after the nurses had cleaned him up.

"He's resting now, but he was awake earlier," the nurse said. "Are you family?"

"No, no, he's a client of mine. I'm a private investigator," Fernando said.

The nurse gave him a funny look. "Okay. The doctor will be in shortly."

'Shortly' turned out to be within the half hour. When he arrived, the doctor looked like he hadn't slept in a week. A dark-haired young man, he had bags under his eyes and two days of dark stubble on his face that added to his exhausted look.

"Sorry to keep you waiting," the doctor said.

Fernando nodded. "No problem."

"Looks like AFib," the doctor said, siding up to Wayne's bed. "Atrial fibrillation. We put him on Coumadin, a blood thinner, and this evening we'll add a channel blocker. That should control the irregular heartbeat. If he remains stable overnight, we'll probably release him tomorrow afternoon. If he's stable."

"Okay," Fernando said.

"Does he have any family in the area?" the doctor asked. "He may need help when he goes home."

"Not that I'm aware of. Just friends," Fernando said.

"Hmmm," the doctor said. "You might want to get him some help. At least a home nurse to stop by every so often to check his vitals and his ability to function on his own. They can give you a number to call at the front counter."

"Okay, thanks," Fernando said.

The doctor turned to leave and then stopped. "By the way, what happened to his fingers? We removed the dirty bandages. Looks like someone had been taking blood samples."

"No idea," Fernando said.

After the doctor left the room, Fernando took a closer look at the cuts in Wayne's fingers. The doctor's question lingered in the room. Who made the cuts--and why?

9

After leaving the hospital, Fernando drove down to Saint Francis Drive and around to the Paseo. He wanted to stop by the *Independent* office on Marcy Street to check with Fidel and find out if there was any more news about the so-called vampire killer. He turned right on Grant Avenue to Marcy, noticing a crowd of protestors surrounding City Hall on the next street over, Lincoln Avenue. You hardly ever saw a scene like this in wealthy Santa Fe, which in recent years had been reshaped by Sotheby's into a playground for the rich and famous.

The demonstrators made Fernando forget about the vampire killer. He pulled over in a parking space on Marcy and walked down Lincoln into a loud, unruly crowd. Most of the protestors were older, well-heeled Santa Feans, not the usual young hooligans you'd expect. Some of them carried signs with slogans such as "Immigrants Go Home," "Clean up our Streets," and "Flush them Out." Looked like at least thirty or forty people, about as many as he'd seen the other day on the Plaza. He plowed through the mob, looking for any sign of a police presence. He thought he saw Sargent Antonio Blake up ahead.

As he neared City Hall Fernando saw Homer Tryzinski talking to a group of people gathered around the front steps. Three toughs stood directly behind Tryzinski. The pugnacious little man had his own posse of bodyguards, all three of them wearing open carry holsters on their hips. Tryzinski gestured angrily with both hands, explaining something to the onlookers. Fernando couldn't make out what Tryzinski was saying because everyone seemed to be talking and chanting at once. The noise level had become deafening.

Just then Fernando spotted an elderly man crossing Lincoln Avenue from Federal Park. The old man looked familiar. He recognized the stocking cap and army jacket: Old Bill from the Fort Marcy homeless camp. Fernando figured Old Bill was making his way down to the Plaza, where he panhandled most afternoons, and decided to check out the ruckus at City Hall.

Old Bill jaywalked across Lincoln Avenue and stepped up on the sidewalk. As soon as he did the three toughs accompanying Tryzinski rushed over to stop him from coming any closer. They pushed him back off the sidewalk and laughed as Old Bill fell on the street, landing on his ass. Old Bill yelped and cursed at the thugs, who continued to laugh at him.

"Hey—-leave him alone," Fernando said, walking up to the guy who'd pushed Old Bill, a short, stocky man who looked like a bulldog, except uglier, with a fat face and hanging jowls, a little too long in the tooth for this kind of work.

"Who's gonna stop me?" bulldog asked. He balled his fists and threw a straight right at Fernando.

Fernando blocked the punch with his left arm, took a step forward, and drove his right hand up into the man's gut as hard as he could.

The man doubled over, gasping for breath.

Fernando brought his knee up under the man's chin and sent him flying backwards on the sidewalk.

Suddenly the other two bodyguards grabbed Fernando and started to smack him with their free hands.

"Enough!" barked someone behind them, shoving through the crowd as he approached.

Fernando recognized Antonio's booming voice. He was never so glad to see the big man. The ex-Marine stood six feet eight inches and weighed two hundred eighty pounds of muscle. As the Santa Fe Police Department's enforcer, no one in their right mind would cross Antonio. He had hands as big as a catcher's mitt and a no tolerance policy for punks.

"You hear me, motherfucker?" Antonio bellowed, grabbing the nearest of the two bodyguards by the shirt collar, lifting him off the ground, and tossing him down flat on his back. The other bodyguard reached for his holster and then thought better of it as Antonio grabbed him by the shoulder and said, "You touch that weapon and I'll break your arm."

While bulldog sat on the ground trying to stop his nosebleed, the other two bodyguards cowered back into the crowd. Away from Antonio, who stood scowling at them.

Now Tryzinski, seeing the confrontation, hurried over to the sidewalk. "What's going on here? My boys were just trying to keep the peace."

Antonio stepped in Tryzinski's face, a good foot taller than the pugnacious little man. "No they weren't. If any of you troublemakers touch another person, I'll arrest you. Understand?"

Tryzinski's face turned red. He wasn't used to being spoken to in such a manner. He turned and walked away.

"Thanks, Antonio," Fernando said.

Antonio smiled. "Just like old times."

"We were a hell of a team," Fernando said.

"Still are," Antonio said. The big man saluted and walked away.

Fernando looked around for Old Bill. The old timer was no longer in the street where he'd fallen. Instead, Old Bill was walking with a slight limp across the grass in Federal Park, heading in the general direction of the Plaza.

Eager to get away from all the noise, Fernando cut over to Marcy Street and walked up to the *Independent* office. A young woman he'd never seen greeted him at the front counter.

"Can I help you?" she asked, a mousy little woman with short-cropped hair and bangs. She eyed him suspiciously.

Suddenly it dawned on Fernando that he looked like a wild man, or like he'd just come from a brawl. His face was red and his shirt was an eyesore, with its shirttail out and its collar torn.

"I'm here to see Fidel," Fernando said weakly, pointing to Fidel sitting in the newsroom typing at his keyboard. He walked into the newsroom before the woman could say anything.

Fidel saw Fernando and waved back at him. "Hey, Fernando."

Fernando took an empty office chair from another desk and pulled it alongside Fidel's. "Don't worry. I'm not here to ask about Take Back Our Streets. I'm more interested in this so-called vampire killer you guys are writing about. Any more developments?"

Fidel nodded. "Yeah, as a matter of fact I'm working on a follow-up right now. A woman contacted me this morning. She works as a server at Chez Paul on Canyon Road. She said she left the restaurant about eleven o'clock last night and was walking to her car when she saw something moving in the trees along the river. She described it as a person or maybe an animal that had a red, bloated face with black markings. She said it stopped and looked at her, so she ran to her car parked on the street and drove away. Said she was scared out of her wits and couldn't sleep last night. Then she decided to call us this morning."

"Any more details?" Fernando asked. "That's not much of a description."

Fidel shook his head. "Not much, because remember it was in the trees about two hundred feet away. She mentioned only one other thing: that the creature was two-legged but looked too heavy to be human. Whatever that means."

Fernando considered. None of it made sense to him. "If the creature was two-legged, what the hell could it be if not human?"

Fidel ignored Fernando's question.

"The red face was the one thing she remembered most vividly," Fidel said. "She said the face looked like it was on fire."

"On fire?"

Fidel nodded.

"Sounds crazy," Fernando said. "Maybe she was drinking at the restaurant?"

"Maybe," Fidel said.

"How about giving me her telephone number or email address?" Fernando said. "Maybe she would remember more details if I told her about what Wayne claimed he saw on Canyon Road."

Fidel shook his head. "No, I really can't give you her contact information. Journalism ethics and all."

"Okay, then how about this," Fernando said, handing Fidel a business card. "Give her my name and number and tell her I'd like to ask her some questions about what she saw. If she's willing. That way she would be the one to initiate the contact."

"Fine. I can do that," Fidel said. "Anything else?"

Fernando laughed. "Sure. Tell your photographers to get me a photo of this vampire or Devil or whatever the hell it is, okay?"

"Now that would sell some newspapers!" Fidel said.

10

Fernando left the *Independent* and walked down Marcy Street to his Cherokee. He noticed the demonstrators were beginning to disperse at City Hall. He wanted nothing more to do with the Take Back Our Streets bunch, so he drove to the Paseo and around to Canyon Road intending to stop at his office. But as he approached the parking lot he changed his mind and kept going. He wanted to check out something Wayne had said right before he collapsed.

Wayne claimed he'd seen and followed the Devil and that he'd been held captive in a shed. If that truly happened, a big if, the shed would have to be in walking distance of Wayne's house since Wayne had no means of transportation other than his own two legs. Furthermore, Wayne left the door open and the radio turned on when he walked out of his house, which meant he intended to be back shortly. While Wayne was recovering in the hospital, this would be a good time to check out the shed story.

Further up Canyon Road Fernando turned into the alley he remembered from his previous visit, thanks to its rustic wooden fence on the left side of the alley. He drove past the row of rusted garbage cans, after which the alley curved up a slight hill to Wayne's pink-colored adobe guesthouse. The place looked the same, with a scattering of cast-off furniture and discarded art supplies littering the dirt yard. Except the front door was closed this time.

So where would Wayne have walked to a shed? That was the question.

Fernando took his binoculars out of the glove compartment and climbed out of the Cherokee. He followed a dirt path up the small hill behind Wayne's adobe, past the picnic table to a flat meadow where he had a clear view of the surroundings. Using his binoculars, he searched for sheds that would be in walking distance of an old timer like Wayne. He saw about a dozen sheds up and down Canyon Road, including one directly across the street from Wayne's alley and another near the old Forest Service building in the foothills of the Sangre de Cristo Mountains. Too many for him to search, even if he knew what he was searching for. The Devil?

Fernando laughed out loud, shaking his head. Why was he even considering this nonsense? He cursed under his breath, disappointed in himself.

He walked back to his Cherokee and decided to check out Wayne's adobe. He found the front door locked, so he took out his lock pick and invited himself in. If anything, the tiny house looked even more crowded than before. On the small table between the two stuffed chairs he saw a revolver and a tattered box of ammunition. The gun turned out to be an old black Army Colt 1911, a museum piece. Which begged the question: what the hell was Wayne doing with an old Colt .45? Was he intending to shoot the Devil? If so, why hadn't he taken his gun with him?

Then Fernando saw something else on the easel in back, a new painting. He walked through piles of trash to the easel, which held a small dark painting of what looked like a mountain sunset. He switched on the nearby light to see better and found himself staring at a painting of a red/brown sky over blue mountains. Even more surprising he noticed a row of tin trays alongside a pile of blood stained towels on the table next to the easel. Among the trays and towels were several used razor blades coated with a dark liquid. That gave him pause. He stood back staring at the razor blades and bloody towels, confused.

Had Wayne cut himself while painting? Why did he have razor blades with his painting supplies? It made no damn sense. None at all.

Suddenly Fernando felt light-headed. The smell of the place was making him sick. Today it stank not only of garbage, but what smelled like a backed-up sewer.

He turned off the light and hurried outside, breathing the fresh air deep into his lungs. The fresh air helped. He climbed into his Cherokee and sat there thinking for a few minutes. Finally he started the engine and drove back down Canyon Road. He bypassed his office and instead turned into El Farol's parking lot a few blocks further down. Getting out of the Cherokee he spotted Dave Stein and another old timer he didn't recognize sitting at one of the small tables on the porch.

Fernando crossed the street and stepped up on the porch. "Did you know that Wayne's in the hospital?"

Dave looked at him. "Who?"

"Never mind," Fernando said, walking into El Farol.

Ruby and Blaine were sitting at a table in the restaurant part of El Farol. Behind them the colorful flamenco dancers in the wall mural seemed to cast them in bright blue and green colors. Arguing as usual, both of them ignored Fernando when he walked over to their table.

"Fuck you, Blaine," Ruby said. "I'm not giving you the last of Jimmy's paintings. He left them to me, remember? Not you."

"Yeah, but wait a minute," Blaine bellowed. "I've sold all of Jimmy's paintings so far, the tourist shit and his Chopped Nudes. We had an arrangement, me and Jimmy."

"Well, you don't have one with me," Ruby shot back, taking notice of Fernando. "What do you think, Fernando?"

"Not my area," Fernando said. "But Jesus, Blaine, haven't you made enough money off Jimmy? You jacked up your prices when he was murdered--you sensationalized the murder as much as possible."

"Damn right!" Ruby added. "He still has that banner in front of his gallery: 'The Last Paintings of the Late, Great, Jimmy Mackey'. Gimme a break."

"Hah! You got your cut, too. I didn't hear you complain then."

"Oh, fuck you, Blaine," Ruby repeated. "You had that banner up before Jimmy was even in the ground."

"So? You gotta strike while the iron is hot," Blaine said.

Ruby laughed and turned to Fernando. "You see what a jackass he is."

Blaine smacked the table with his big palm. "You're a hard woman to do business with, Ruby. Hell, let's have another round."

With that Blaine stood up and shouted to Jack, the bartender: "Margaritas all around, Jacko! ASAP!"

Ruby rolled her eyes.

Fernando shrugged and took a seat at the table. "Hey, you guys are supposed to be friends."

"Hah!" Ruby said.

When Janice, the waitress, brought the drinks, Blaine said, "Thanks, darling!"

Janice gave him the Evil Eye and left Blaine the check.

Blaine turned to Fernando. "So what are you doing here? I didn't know private eyes started drinking so early?"

"Only when we need to," Fernando said. "I wanted to run something by you and get your opinion. It's about Wayne--he's in the hospital."

Both Ruby and Blaine stared at him.

Fernando told them about having to call an ambulance for Wayne and about what he'd found that afternoon in Wayne's house, the razor blades and bloody towels.

Ruby shook her head. "Sounds like Wayne. He probably cut himself while he was trying to cut and mix his paints or God knows what. He has dementia, what do you expect?"

Blaine was uncharacteristically silent.

Fernando turned to Blaine.

Blaine shrugged and raised his margarita. "Don't know and don't care."

11

Fernando walked into his office next morning only to find his desk phone ringing off the hook. It stopped ringing by the time he switched the sign on his window from 'Closed' to 'Open.' Then it started ringing again the second he sat down at his desk, trying to clear his head from the margaritas he'd consumed yesterday at El Farol. Blaine and Ruby could drink margaritas all evening, but he couldn't. For the thousandth time he made a mental note to never have anything stronger than his usual Modelo.

Finally he picked up the phone, just to stop the ringing. "Yeah?"

"Uh...Lopez...where the hell are you?" a voice croaked at the other end.

Fernando's spirits sank. It was only ten o'clock and already the day was in the crapper. "What do you want, Wayne?"

"I want you to come pick me up, what do you think...I just got my walking papers."

Fernando rubbed his forehead and shook his head to think clearly. "Why don't you call Blaine?"

"It was you who brought me to this damn hospital," Wayne said. "And anyway, I already called Blaine and he told me to piss off...the sonofabitch. I got nobody else to call...and you're responsible for this."

"You collapsed in my office," Fernando said. "I had to call nine one one to revive you."

Silence at the other end.

"Your heart stopped, you weren't breathing," Fernando added.

"So you called an ambulance? I got no money to pay for that."

Fernando sighed. "Just forget about the money. The hospital will help you apply for Medicaid, if you don't already have it."

"Okay...pick me up at the Emergency Room door," Wayne said and hung up before Fernando could say no.

Fernando slammed down the phone, resisting the urge to grab it and throw it against the wall. Calm down, he told himself. Wayne just wants a ride home. Pick him up and drop him off at his adobe. No big deal.

It was Fernando's own damn fault anyway. If he'd thrown Wayne out of his office the first time he'd shown up talking about the Devil, none of this would have happened.

His head throbbed now, thanks to the combination of Wayne and last night's margaritas. He found a bottle of Tylenol in his desk drawer and popped two tablets. Then he locked up and walked to his Cherokee.

Fernando drove slowly, trying to relax. By the time he reached Christus Saint Vincent Hospital on Saint Michael's Drive he'd calmed down some. Calm enough to feel a twinge of compassion when he saw Wayne sitting in a wheelchair outside the Emergency Room. Wayne wore a clean set of clothes, a plaid shirt and khaki pants, while holding a bulky plastic bag in his lap, probably his old black suit. At the moment Wayne was trying to swat away the nurse helping him. The nurse was having none of Wayne's nonsense. Instead, she grabbed hold of the push handles and shook the chair in order to get him to stop swatting her.

Fernando turned into the loading area in front of the Emergency Room and idled. He'd be damned if he would get out of the Cherokee.

Wayne waved at Fernando and climbed out of the wheelchair without waiting for the nurse to help him. He hobbled across the sidewalk to the Cherokee and then fumbled with the door handle. Once inside the Cherokee he barked, "'Bout time...I've been waiting near two hours!"

Fernando gave him a dirty look. "So what happened to you the other day? I saw the bloody towels and razor blades at your house yesterday. Did you cut yourself?"

Wayne stared straight ahead. "Don't know what you're talking about."

"And what about the story you told about being locked in a shed?" Fernando asked. "Where was this shed? And who locked you in?"

"Never you mind, Lopez," Wayne said. "I don't remember saying anything like that. I wasn't feeling too good back then...light-headed and dizzy...I might have said some things I shouldn't have said, I don't know. I don't remember a goddamn thing 'till I woke up in the hospital."

Fernando nodded, turning onto the Paseo and then right on Canyon Road. He had to wonder. Was Wayne having memory problems typical of someone with dementia, or was he lying? And if he was lying, why was he lying?

Fernando drove up the alley to Wayne's adobe and pulled up in front. "You want me to come in? Help out?"

"Hell no, I don't need your help," Wayne said and opened the door of the Cherokee.

"Here," Fernando said, handing Wayne a brochure he'd picked up at the Emergency Room. "Information about enrolling in a program where a nurse visits you from time to time to make sure you're okay."

Wayne stuffed the brochure in his pocket and climbed out of the Cherokee.

Fernando watched Wayne hobble to his front door and disappear inside.

Good riddance.

Fernando put the Cherokee in gear and drove back down to Canyon Road. At the end of the alley he stopped to consider his options. He could call Antonio or Ruby to see if either one of them wanted to meet for lunch. Except Antonio would want to meet at the Shed and expect him to pay, and Ruby would want to meet at El Farol and order drinks, the last thing he needed this morning. So he decided to go home for lunch.

Fernando drove down Canyon Road to the Paseo and around to Acequia Madre. On Acequia Madre his sweet little adobe was tucked away among the million dollar mansions the newcomers had built or remodeled. He took great pride in his 1920s adobe, which stuck out like a sore thumb on Santa Fe's fashionable East side. He'd taken great pains to preserve the house just as it was when he and Estelle bought it when they were first married. Fuck gentrification.

He pulled into his driveway and walked into his kitchen, with windows and doors painted turquoise blue to keep away the evil spirits. Taking no chances, Estelle had even painted the kitchen cabinets blue.

Estelle usually took her lunch to work, so he had the house to himself. He made himself a quick sandwich and took it outside on their patio to eat. Why eat inside on a day as fine as this? The tail end of summer, or the beginning of fall depending on how you looked at it, was his favorite time of year. Crisp blue skies, lots of sunshine, and fresh mountain air. The tall cottonwoods along the acequia were almost ready to turn, their leaves tinted with yellow. The sweet smell of Piñon smoke would soon be in the air, wafting out of chimneys along the street.

After finishing his lunch he locked up and drove back to his office on Canyon Road. He found the parking lot crowded with out-of state-cars, which would make Ruby happy next door. More traffic meant more business for her gallery. He parked the Cherokee in his reserved space and walked down the path to his office, located down a slight hill and behind Ruby's gallery.

Once inside he checked his messages and found nothing of interest, only a sales call from a home security outfit that wanted to sell him an alarm. He put his feet up on his desk and picked up the day's *Independent*, which he'd brought from home but hadn't had time to read this morning. He finished the sports news and was about to read the front section when he noticed a shadow approaching his door. He put down the newspaper and waited.

The shadow turned out to be a woman. She opened the door without knocking, a thirty-something woman with long black hair and glasses. He noticed she had one of his business cards in hand.

"Mister Lopez?" she asked.

"That's me. What can I do for you?"

"I got your card from Fidel Rodriguez at the *Independent*," she said. "I don't know if you've seen the story he wrote about me in today's paper, but he said you wanted to talk to me about what I saw. I'm Crystal Montoya, by the way."

Fernando shook his head. "I haven't seen the story yet, but yes, come in. Have a seat."

She sat in the chair facing the desk, still holding his business card. "Mister Rodriguez said you wanted to know if I could think of any more details," she said.

Fernando nodded.

"Well, I pretty much told him everything. I'd just gotten off work and was walking down Canyon Road to my car when I saw something red moving in the trees down by the river. Like I told Mister Rodriguez, at first I thought it was a wounded animal––you know, bleeding. Then it suddenly stopped. It turned and looked at me and seemed to fix me in its vision. That's when I realized I was looking at the face of a two-legged creature about to attack me. I got scared and ran to my car and drove off without looking back. I couldn't sleep all night thinking about it, so the next morning I called the *Independent* and talked to Mister Rodriguez."

"Okay, but can you describe the face?" Fernando asked. "What did it look like? I'm asking for more details."

Crystal shivered. "I hate to even think about that face. It was blood red, round as a pumpkin. Looked like it was made out of melting wax. With big black eyes hollowed out."

"But you think it was human," Fernando said.

She shrugged. "The form of a human, anyway."

"What do you mean when you say the face looked like melting wax? I don't understand."

"It's hard to explain," she said. "I mean like blood bleeding out of the red face."

"That's it?" Fernando asked. "That's all you have?"

"That's all," Crystal said. "Except maybe for one thing. I thought I heard a humming sound coming from the trees."

"A humming sound?"

"Yeah, like 'mmmmm' or something like that."

When Fernando didn't respond, she asked, "Do you think what I saw was the vampire killer?"

Fernando laughed, in spite of himself. "I have no idea what it was you saw, but if you see it again, give me a call. And don't hesitate. Call me right away."

12

After Crystal left his office, Fernando finished reading the *Independent*, including Fidel's news story on the so-called vampire killer. More sensationalism, typical of the *Independent*. He wondered how Fidel, one of his oldest and most responsible friends, could write such nonsense. He tossed the newspaper in the trash and checked the time: half past four. Closing time.

He decided to check on Wayne before going home, just to make sure the old fool was okay. He felt somehow responsible for Wayne, though he didn't know exactly why. After all, Wayne wasn't a paying client. In fact, Wayne had been a thorn in his side ever since he retired and set up shop on Canyon Road. So why now? He supposed it had something to do with Wayne's involvement in this story of a Devil or vampire loose in Santa Fe. His instincts told him that Wayne could be the key in getting to the bottom of this craziness.

Fernando hung the 'Closed' sign in his door and locked up for the night. Outside the parking lot was nearly empty, the tourists having thinned out as the afternoon cooled. An unseasonably cold wind blew out of the north, hinting at the change of season to come. Fiesta madness would start soon, too soon. He climbed into his Cherokee and drove up Canyon Road, turning right into the now familiar alley. He saw no sign of activity as he parked in front of Wayne's tumbledown adobe.

Fernando walked to the front door and knocked. When no one answered, he helped himself and found the door unlocked. Inside looked much the same. "Wayne? Where are you?" he asked.

He heard a rustling sound in the back bedroom, which sounded like mice scratching on baseboards. Still, he was cautious. He eased over to the wall and looked into the room. Piled on the bed were mounds of dirty clothes and blankets. The bedside bureau was buried under a stack of dishes and drinking glasses. Looked like Wayne ate his meals in bed.

Once again the stench of filth and perspiration overwhelmed him, so much so that he staggered out bumping into Wayne's easel.

Fernando cursed as Wayne's painting of a red sky crashed to the floor. He lifted the painting and put it back on the easel, noticing it hadn't progressed since his last visit. The bloody rags and razor blades he'd seen earlier remained on the side table, as before.

So where was Wayne? Once again the old fool had disappeared.

Fernando hurried outside to escape the pungent smell. He leaned against his Cherokee, breathing the fresh air and considering what to do next. He happened to notice a footpath winding around the adobe and up to the old Forest Service building in the foothills. The well-worn dirt path spiked his curiosity. He left the side of his Cherokee and walked to the path, finding a myriad of footprints going up and down the hill. He had no other leads as to Wayne's whereabouts, so he took a chance and started walking up the slope.

The trail curved through a sagebrush meadow sprinkled with cholla and prickly pear cactus and occasional white and blue wildflowers. It took him a good fifteen minutes to reach the timberline walking at a leisurely but steady pace. As he approached the building he noticed the lone figure of a woman working in a small vegetable garden in front, next to a flagpole sans flag. Behind her a two-story log A-frame with a wrap-around porch towered over the woman. Off to the side stood another building, a small shed. The shed's wooden door was open, revealing rakes, shovels, pickaxes, and other tools stacked and propped up along the sides of the shed.

Remembering Wayne's story about being locked in a shed, Fernando made an effort to scour the interior of the slat and plywood shed as he walked by. Didn't look like the kind of structure that would lend itself for use as a prison. Much too flimsy.

The woman stopped working when she saw him approaching, an attractive middle-aged woman with short black hair wearing jeans and a black T-shirt. She smiled, tentatively, holding a metal bowl filled with tomatoes and lettuce from her garden.

"¡Hola," she said, fidgeting with her bowl.

"Howdy," Fernando replied. "Sorry to bother you, I'm looking for an old man who's disappeared. He's in his eighties, with white hair and beard. Last time I saw him he was wearing a plaid shirt and khaki pants."

The woman continued to fidget with her bowl.

"He lives in that house down there," Fernando said, pointing to

Wayne's adobe at the bottom of the hill. "He gets confused sometimes. I think he may have wandered off this afternoon."

The woman shook her head. "No, we rent...we no see anyone here."

Fernando introduced himself and handed her a business card. "If you see an old man who looks like Santa Claus, please give me a call," he said, laughing.

"Si," she said, glancing at the A-frame behind her, as if expecting someone to come to her rescue.

Fernando looked over the aging wooden structure, its logs discolored by mold or wood rot in spots. Its dark windows looked like they hadn't been cleaned in years.

"Nice garden," Fernando said, motioning to her garden. "How long have you lived here?"

"We come this summer," she said, in a heavy Spanish accent.

Fernando nodded. "You and your husband?"

"Si, and my husband brother," the woman said. "My name's Maria Aragon, my husband Ricardo. He's a painter."

"Oh, is he here now?" Fernando asked, moving toward the A-frame.

Maria moved to stop him. "No, no, he is painting now. No can be disturbed."

"I understand," Fernando aid. "Maybe some other time. Would you mind if I took a look around a bit, just to see if my friend wandered off into the foothills?"

Maria glanced at the A-frame again. "Okay."

"Thanks," Fernando said, and made his way around the vegetable garden. Parked alongside the house was a white VW camper van with a Chihuahua, Mexico license plate.

The license plate explained the woman's accent. They were from Mexico. That didn't bother Fernando. Santa Fe was a sanctuary city, with a fair number of immigrants from south of the border, some legal, some illegal. He didn't give a damn if they were legal or not. Every single person now living in Santa Fe was an immigrant. Last time he checked the original Ogapoge Pueblo and its descendants were long gone, victims of history.

Fernando didn't expect to find Wayne hiding among the juniper and ponderosa pine. He was hoping to find a side window in the A-frame that would allow him to see inside. To get a look at Ricardo, Maria's husband, and whoever else might be inside.

Maria's nervousness bothered Fernando. What was she tying to hide? Maybe they were squatters and not actually renting the A-frame. At any rate, if Wayne didn't turn up, he would have to come back with Manny or Antonio.

He saw nothing of interest in the VW camper. When he walked back to the garden he noticed the woman had disappeared, probably into the A-frame.

He had an urge to knock on the door but decided against it. Instead he headed back down the footpath to his Cherokee.

Walking down was easier than walking up the hill. It took only a few minutes to reach Wayne's adobe. When he came to his Cherokee and opened the door he happened to notice that Wayne's door was partially open. The door had been closed earlier. He quietly reached over the seat and took out his Smith and Wessen from the glove compartment. Not knowing who or what had entered the adobe, he wanted to be prepared.

Fernando crept up to the door and opened it slowly. He saw no one in the large open room but heard a sound coming from the back bedroom. He eased into the room and listened. The sound was louder now, a wheezing sound. Holding his Smith & Wessen in front of him, he crept across the room to the door of the bedroom and looked inside. There, lying on the bed amid piles of blankets and dirty clothes, was none other than Wayne. Wheezing and snoring and otherwise sound asleep.

Cursing, Fernando put down his Smith & Wessen and walked quickly out of the small adobe. What was he thinking? Of course Wayne would show up unexpectedly. He was damn tired of taking care of the old fool. Let him take care of himself.

13

After breakfast the next morning Fernando decided to stop by the Washington Avenue Station to check with Manny. He wanted to know more about the man injured during the raid on the homeless camp in Fort Marcy Park. The one Old Bill knocked unconscious. Specifically, he wanted to know who the guy was and who he worked for. So he drove around the Paseo to Marcy Street and found a parking spot near the coffee shop. He no longer had his reserved spot in the station parking lot, so he was forced to plug a meter like a common, ordinary tourist. Luckily it was early so the damned tourists hadn't taken all the spaces.

Fernando walked down Washington Avenue and into the station, where his friend Linda greeted him from behind the front counter. "Ah-ha, I knew you wouldn't be able to stay away. Fess up, you miss us, Fernando!"

Fernando laughed. "I miss you, anyway. That's more than I can say for some of my former colleagues."

Linda smiled, knowing about his troubled history with the Chief. She whispered, "Yeah, the Chief misses you too."

"He misses his whipping boy, does he?"

"Seriously, I think he does miss you because now he has to deal with Manny," Linda said. "You know Manny."

Fernando laughed. "The two of them deserve each other. Speaking of Manny, is he in his office?"

Linda nodded as the phone rang and she reached for the receiver.

Fernando walked down the hall to what had been his office before he retired. The office looked exactly the same: dark, with heavy blinds on the window, dreary metal furniture, and paperwork scattered over every surface. Manny sat at his desk scrolling down on his cell phone.

"What a dump," Fernando said, taking a seat in a metal chair beside the desk.

Manny smiled. "Yeah, I kept it just the way you left it––the grunge look."

Looking around the office Fernando felt a twinge of nostalgia, but it passed quickly. "So what's the latest on the guy Old Bill knocked unconscious in Fort Marcy Park?"

"He's brain dead," Manny said. "No brain waves. They're gonna pull the plug this afternoon."

"Who is he?"

Manny shook his head. "No one knows. He's been working as a dishwasher at Tryzinski's restaurant, Homer's Diner. We know this because we were able to identity one of the other thugs who broke up the camp. This guy told us he worked with the dead guy at Homer's Diner. He told us he didn't know who the dead guy was or where he lived, only that he was from Mexico and spoke very little English."

"Talk about irony," Fernando said. "Tryzinski's own restaurant hires illegal immigrants. What happened to 'Take Back Our Streets'?"

"No shit," Manny said. "Of course, Tryzinski claimed he'd never met the dead guy, that all hiring at his restaurant is done by the restaurant manager, who is conveniently on vacation somewhere in Southern California, according to Tryzinski."

Fernando nodded. "Did you bring in Old Bill for questioning?"

Manny made a face. "No. I asked the Chief if he wanted me to bring in Bill for a statement. He laughed at me and said, 'For a fucking illegal who we can't even identify--get real.' Then he walked away."

Fernando sighed. "Sounds like the Chief."

"No name, no rights, no life, just another illegal," Manny said. "Pull the plug and throw him in a pauper's grave."

"Yeah, and another illegal dishwasher Tryzinski could hire at sub-minimum wages," Fernando added. "What a fucking hypocrite!"

Manny nodded. "Yep, it's a joke, the whole 'Take Back' thing. They target the poor schmucks who come in to work for peanuts instead of the drug cartels that have made fentanyl the national snack. The Sinaloa Cartel has been active in Albuquerque for years, now they're moving into Santa Fe. Just last week a lowly runner was bringing in a shipment of fentanyl when he came off Interstate Twenty-Five too fast and plowed into the rear of another car on Cerrillos Road. When the cops got there he was running down the street with two suitcases filled with Mexican Blues."

Fernando started to ask what happened to the runner when Manny raised his hand. "Don't even ask. Before we could get him to talk, he was found hanging from the ceiling of his jail cell with a sheet around his neck."

Fernando shook his head.

"The Sinaloa crowd has a long reach," Manny said.

"So what other uplifting news do you have for me this morning?" Fernando asked, smiling.

"That's about it, my friend," Manny said. "There's a 'Take Back Our Streets' rally this weekend. We're supposed to provide security, just in case some troublemakers show up."

Fernando laughed. "I thought they were the troublemakers."

Manny smiled. "You're developing a sense of humor, Fernando.

"Comes with being retired."

"I can't wait," Manny said. "Sadly, I have twenty more years of this shit."

"Goes by fast," Fernando said, wistfully. He stood up and said, "Keep me informed."

"Will do," Manny said as Fernando walked out of the office.

Once outside, Fernando walked back to Marcy Street. He climbed into his Cherokee and drove up to the Paseo and over to Canyon Road, already crawling with tourists. He pulled into his parking lot and parked alongside Ruby's Honda Accord. On his way to his office he noticed Ruby and Blaine talking inside the front windows of Ruby's gallery. Looked like they were arguing, as usual. He saw Blaine throw up his hands in disgust and yell something at Ruby. Ruby returned the favor and added a little sign language: her finger.

Fernando decided to stop by the gallery first before going to his office, so he walked up the steps to the porch and opened the door. "Do you two ever stop arguing?" he asked.

"Hell no," Ruby said, wearing a tight black dress that made her look twenty years younger. "He's still bugging me about selling the last of Jimmy's paintings, and I told him to fuck off. I'm selling Jimmy's paintings. I was married to the asshole!"

"You were married to him for less than a year," Blaine said. "I was the one who put up with him all these years trying to sell his paintings, which wasn't easy," Blaine replied.

Ruby shrugged.

Today Blaine wore a loud turquoise colored Hawaiian shirt over his red Bermuda shorts. "And let's face it, you can't sell paintings here because this is just a pottery gallery!" Blaine added.

"What do you mean 'just a pottery gallery'?" Ruby shot back, pissed.

"You've had them for two years now, and how many have you sold? Nada! Not a fucking one of them!"

"So? Why should I give you twenty percent when I can sell them here and get one hundred percent? Answer me that."

Blaine turned to Fernando. "You see this? Dealing with her is just as bad as dealing with Jimmy. Fucking crazy, both of them!"

"Oh, fuck you, Blaine," Ruby said to the big man, who was a good foot and a half taller than her.

"Fine! To hell with it then," Blaine said, shaking his head. "I've found a new artist I want to feature anyway. A Mexican painter who's staying in Santa Fe. He's the real deal."

"Who's that?" Ruby asked, skeptical.

"Guy by the name of Ricardo Aragon," Blaine said. "He's doing some interesting stuff. I took several of his paintings and got him to sign a contract."

The name caught Fernando by surprise. "Ricardo Aragon? I met his wife yesterday."

"No way!" Blaine bellowed.

"Yes, I ran into her while I was looking for Wayne on Upper Canyon Road," Fernando said. He explained that he'd stopped by Wayne's adobe to check on him but found the house empty, so he'd walked up the trail to the old Forest Service building at the edge of the national forest, where he saw Maria Aragon working in her garden.

"You mean that old A-frame?" Ruby asked.

Fernando nodded. "Maria said they were renting it. I didn't meet her husband. She said he was inside painting."

"Yeah, best to not disturb him, I need more of his work," Blaine said. "And this guy's the real deal."

Ruby frowned. "So you keep saying."

"What's that supposed to mean?" Blaine asked.

Fernando raised his hand. "Peace."

Ruby checked her watch. "Happy Hour's just starting at El Farol. You guys wanna go?"

"I thought you'd never ask," Blaine said.

Shaking his head, Fernando followed them.

14

Fernando had just finished watching the ten o'clock news when his cell phone rang. Who would be calling this late at night? He first thought it might be one of his daughters, Flavia or Adela. Probably Flavia, who lived with her husband Luis in Tesuque. Adela lived in Las Vegas and usually only called on weekends. Either way he feared the worst, since people generally didn't call this late at night except for bad news and emergencies.

He didn't recognize the number when he picked up the phone. "Lopez here," he said.

"Mr. Lopez, it's Crystal," Came an out-of-breath voice. "It's back... the red face...in the trees. I ran down to my car. I'm driving away now. You asked me to call you if I saw it again."

"Where are you now?" Fernando asked.

"Driving down Canyon Road," Crystal said. "I saw it in the trees just up the street from Chez Paul. Near the El Farol parking lot."

"Just now?" he asked.

"Yes, right now!" she nearly screamed.

"Okay, thanks, I'm on my way," Fernando said and clicked off.

Fernando grabbed his Smith & Wessen and rushed out of the house without telling Estelle, who was already getting ready for bed. He figured he would be back before she noticed his absence. She often went to bed first and was sound asleep when he joined her.

Fernando jumped in his Cherokee and raced around the Paseo to Canyon Road. He slowed down approaching Chez Paul, scanning the trees along the river. When he pulled into the El Farol parking lot, he cut his engine and climbed out of the Cherokee as quietly as possible. He walked to the rear of the parking lot overlooking the river and waited, looking for any movement. Moonlight created jagged shadows in the yards below and the trees along the river. He heard nothing, saw nothing.

Not waiting, Fernando crept down the hill. He avoided the yards by taking a public path that led down to the river. Somewhere in the distance a dog barked. Overhead the moon moved behind a cloud as he entered the trees, plunging his surroundings into darkness. He stopped briefly, allowing his eyes time to adjust to the darkness. Then he continued moving cautiously through the trees, watching his every step as he navigated the uneven riverbank.

Moments later he thought he heard a twig snap up ahead. Then he heard a low humming sound. He remembered Crystal saying she heard a humming sound when she spotted the creature with the red face.

Fernando froze, unsure of what to do next. Suddenly he realized he'd climbed out of the Cherokee so fast he'd left his Smith & Wessen on the front passenger car seat. What a fool he'd been! He considered turning around and going back to his Cherokee to get his weapon. But by then it might be too late. So he soldiered on, looking for a rock or heavy stick that he could use to defend himself. Soon he came across a j-shaped stick with a curve at the end. That would have to do.

Now the humming stopped.

His heart raced. Was he about to encounter the Devil or the vampire killer? He tried to put such nonsense out of his mind. Not easy to do under the circumstances. In the darkness.

Suddenly the humming started again. This time behind him. And close.

Fernando spun around. A huge red face flashed in front of him. A split instant later a hard object hit the side of his head. The blow sent him reeling to the ground.

His attacker swung again. He felt the air currents ripple over his head.

Desperate, Fernando tried to strike at his attacker with his stick. His attacker, man or beast he couldn't tell, kicked at the stick and stumbled backwards. That gave Fernando enough time to roll down toward the river. He rolled over the muddy lip of the river and splashed in the trickle of water that was the Santa Fe River. Then he clawed his way up the other bank of the river and scrambled up to East Alameda Street. He quickly picked up a softball size rock and turned back to the river, but his attacker hadn't followed him. He heard more humming in the trees on the other side of the river, getting fainter as the creature walked away.

Now what? He took a seat at one of the picnic tables along Alameda to get his wits about him. What had he seen? He couldn't be sure. Whatever it was had a round red face and a black body. That much he was sure of.

He waited until the humming stopped and then walked down to the Delgado Street Bridge and over to Canyon Road. His attacker seemed to shy away from lights, so he walked in the center of the street well illuminated by the streetlights along Canyon Road. He hurried up the street to the El Farol parking lot, encountering no one on the deserted street.

By the time he reached his Cherokee he wasn't so much shaken as pissed. He took his Smith & Wessen out of the Cherokee and walked to the edge of the parking lot looking for his assailant in the trees below. He wasn't about to go back into the trees, so he stood there for a good half hour just waiting for a chance to put a bullet in whoever or whatever it was with the red face if it ventured near the parking lot.

Eventually his anger subsided. He told himself he would have another chance to settle up with his assailant. So he climbed into his Cherokee and drove back around to his house on Acequia Madre, keeping his Smith & Wessen on the passenger's seat just in case he happened to see the red-faced sonofabitch on the way home. He didn't.

Fernando parked at the end of their driveway so as not to disturb Estelle. He took his Smith & Wessen into the house with him. He never left it in the Cherokee, because there were too many young punks breaking into cars these days. The last thing they needed was another gun.

Once inside their adobe, Fernando tip-toed to the hallway bathroom and looked at himself in the mirror. He didn't like what he saw: a wrinkled old man with bags under his eyes and cropped salt and pepper hair, more salt than pepper every time he looked.

The welt on the left side of his face didn't help, giving him a lopsided appearance. Be a nasty bruise, but no blood to clean up anyway.

He washed his face, removed his clothes, and tip-toed down the hallway into their bedroom, where he quietly slipped under the blankets.

"So where have you been?" Estelle asked, taking Fernando by surprise.

14

Nightmares tormented Fernando most of the night. The red faced creature kept appearing unexpectedly in his dreams, no matter if he were fishing at Canjilon Lakes, eating lunch at the Shed, or dancing with Estelle at Flavia's wedding. A big red liquid face that looked like it was pouring or peeling off. As a result he woke up covered in sweat and grumpy as all get out. He sat on the edge of the bed rubbing his eyes, trying to wake up. He had half a notion to get back in bed and sleep for another hour or so, something he rarely did, but the thought of more nightmares overruled that notion.

In contrast, Estelle was already up and dressed and as chipper as usual. She came back to the bedroom before leaving for the day. "Are you getting out of bed or what? I left you some eggs and sausage. You can make your own coffee."

Fernando grunted something inaudible.

Estelle paused for a moment trying to figure out what he'd said and then threw up her arms and walked out of the house. He heard her Camry start up outside and drive away.

Fernando took his time. He splashed water on his face and got dressed. He made himself a small pot of drip coffee and warmed his breakfast in the microwave, adding toast and jam to accompany his second cup of coffee.

Feeling better, he read the morning *Independent* at the kitchen table, looking for news of the vampire killer or the Take Back Our Streets group. He found nothing new, so he locked up and drove around the Paseo to Canyon Road.

By the time Fernando pulled into his parking lot it was nearly ten o'clock. He opened up and checked his messages. Only one message from yesterday evening at 8:05 p.m., a crackly old voice he thought was Wayne until he heard the name: "Lopez...I got something for you...you won't believe this...it's Bill calling, your informant...I saw it, making its way up

Alameda along the river...you better watch your step...you know where to find me."

True, Fernando had used Old Bill as an informant on many occasions. Old Bill seemed to know pretty much everything that transpired on the streets at any given time. Old Bill didn't drink, not much anyway, so he was usually pretty reliable. But what had Old Bill seen on the river? Was it the same thing he had seen last night: the human-like figure with a bright red face?

Fernando made a mental note to check out Old Bill's camp at Fort Marcy Park later that day. Get the whole story.

In the meantime he had work to do on his books, work he'd been postponing for weeks. He hated to look at the numbers because he knew the office was losing money, thanks to his weakness for poor people who needed help, which often prompted him to work *pro bono*. Not good for the books. He'd incurred big expenses staying in Taos on his last two cases, the murders at Painted Skull Ranch and, more recently, the feud in Cabresto Canyon. He hadn't been paid a dime in either case.

Same with this latest case, if it was a case. He had no hope of getting paid for chasing Wayne around Canyon Road or pursuing this creature with a red face. Fortunately Ruby didn't charge him rent to use her garage as an office, but still, something had to give soon or Estelle would start complaining and he would feel like a damned fool.

While he was adding up his losses, Fernando heard someone walk up to his office door. He looked up to see a huge shadow standing outside the door. Then the door opened and Antonio walked in carrying a paper cup of Starbuck's coffee.

"Wanna get some lunch?" Antonio asked.

With his enormous size, Antonio needed huge quantities of food. He was famous for mooching lunches off his colleagues at the Washington Avenue Station. Even though Fernando had been retired for over a year now, Antonio still hit on him at least once a week for a lunch at the Shed, their favorite restaurant, or La Choza, their second favorite restaurant.

"I don't know, what time is it?" Fernando asked, checking his watch.

"Nearly Noon," Antonio said. "I'm starving."

Fernando laughed. "What else is new?"

Antonio took a seat across from the desk, spilling his coffee on the newly carpeted floor. "Shit," the big man said, rubbing the coffee into the brown carpet with a wad of napkins from Starbucks.

"So what's up?" Antonio asked.

Fernando frowned. "I found a message on my phone from Old Bill this morning. He said he saw something on Alameda Street yesterday. Wants me to stop by his camp for the details."

Antonio gave him a strange look. "You haven't heard? Old Bill's dead. Someone beat him to death. A shopkeeper found him in an alley off Marcy Street. Looks like he was on his way back to his camp at Fort Marcy."

Stunned, Fernando didn't know what to say, so he pushed the replay button on his answering machine. They listened in silence to Old Bill's message.

Antonio shook his head. "Jesus! The voice of a dead man. Creeps me out."

"What have you turned up so far?" Fernando asked.

"Somebody went after him using an old fashion meat hammer with a wooden handle, one of those things you use to tenderize meat," Antonio said. "Hit him so hard the wooden handle broke off. Fractured his skull in a couple of places. We haven't heard from Forensics yet, but the cause of death should be no great secret."

Fernando nodded. "Are you thinking the same thing I'm thinking?"

"Yep, I'm thinking it's the same people who raided Old Bill's camp," Antonio said. "The attacker wasn't the smartest guy in town. He left the head of the hammer lying on the ground and tossed the wooden handle in an alley garbage can. Fingerprints and all."

"A kitchen implement," Fernando said, mostly to himself.

Antonio smiled. "Leads us right to Tryzinski and his restaurant. Hopefully to the killer. We found plenty of skin and blood under Old Bill's fingernails. He put up a hell of a fight."

"He was quite a guy," Fernando said, shaking his head. "Tough as nails."

"But not as tough as a meat tenderizer," Antonio joked.

Fernando gave him the Evil Eye.

"So what do you think? The Shed? Or maybe go down to La Choza?"

"Let's go to The Shed, it's closer, "Fernando said.

"As long as you're buying," Antonio said.

Fernando locked up and the two of them climbed into his Cherokee, leaving Antonio's cruiser parked near Ruby's gallery. He drove around to Alameda Street and followed it down past the Paseo to the Cathedral. He found a parking place just south of Shelby Street. On the other side of Alameda, he saw a gathering of homeless people wrapped in blankets sleeping along the Santa Fe River. He'd never seen so many homeless people gathered in one place downtown.

"Won't Tryzinski love this!" Fernando said.

"It's getting worse every week," Antonio said. "Somehow the fucking politicians are going to have to deal with this problem--not just kick these people out or lock them up."

They walked over to Palace and up to the colorful Shed restaurant, its patio painted nearly every color in the rainbow. The tables out front were just beginning to fill up, with tourists as well as locals dedicated to the historic restaurant. Their favorite server, Julie, gave them their usual two-person corner table overlooking the patio. They ordered the same thing they always ordered: Cheese Enchiladas with red chile for Fernando; Combination Plate with both red and green chile for Antonio. Mocha cake times two for dessert.

They were halfway through their meals when Antonio's cell phone rang. "Yeah, I'm eating lunch at the Shed. Why?"

That caught Fernando's attention.

"Okay, I'm on my way," Antonio said. He turned to Fernando. "Eat up. I need to meet Manny at Tryzinski's restaurant on Cerrillos Road. They got a warrant to search the place. You can come along."

15

On their way to Tryzinski's restaurant Fernando told Antonio about encountering the creature with a red face the night before. After leaving the Shed, they'd gone directly to his office and changed vehicles, swapping the Cherokee for Antonio's police cruiser. Now with Antonio at the wheel, they were speeding along Cerrillos Road, the ugly strip of fast food restaurants and cheap motels that cluttered the southern entrance into Santa Fe on Highway 14.

"So this creature with a red face is real?" Antonio asked, after Fernando had finished telling him about how he'd escaped.

Fernando shrugged. It's something. I don't know what."

As they approached the restaurant, named 'Homer's Place' after Tryzinski's first name, they saw Manny's cruiser parked in front of the rectangular brick building, which had a long bank of windows overlooking Cerrillos Road. A red, white, and blue neon sign blinked 'Homer's Place' over the front entrance. On the door jam a small American flag was attached by means of a flag bracket. To Fernando the nondescript building looked like a diner you might find in any suburban strip mall; it might be acceptable out on Cerrillos Road, but it wouldn't be allowed anywhere near Santa Fe's historical district downtown. Too modern, too sterile.

Antonio parked next to Manny's vehicle and then climbed out of his cruiser. He stopped at the front door and motioned for Fernando to stay back. "You can watch, but don't get involved, okay? I don't want to get anyone in trouble."

"No problem," Fernando said. He followed Antonio into the restaurant but stayed by the door. From there he saw Tryzinski standing by the lunch counter talking to Manny and another young cop he didn't know. Manny waved the search warrant in Tryzinski's face, and Tryzinski in turn tried to swat it away. Both men started yelling.

That's when Antonio strolled calmly to the counter and asked,

"What's the problem?"

"This is bullshit, that's what's the problem," Tryzinski said, balling his fists as if he were about to fight. "I'm a businessman. I'm running for City Council."

Manny didn't back down. "We have a warrant to search the place, now get out of the way."

At that point Antonio stepped in Tryzinski's face, towering over the pudgy little man, and said, "You heard the man."

When Tryzinski didn't move, Antonio shoved him out of the way, knocking him back into the counter.

Tryzinski sputtered, trying to control his anger, while Manny and the other cop walked behind the counter into the kitchen.

Tryzinski and Antonio stood glaring at each other.

Soon Fernando heard the sound of objects breaking in the kitchen. Sounded like all hell was breaking loose. Then shouting and loud footsteps.

"We have a runner!" Manny shouted from the kitchen.

Antonio dashed into the kitchen. He ran like a linebacker in the National Football League. For a man his size, he was unbelievably fast.

Tryzinski followed, keeping a safe distance from Antonio.

Fernando brought up the rear. In the kitchen he found two of Tryzinski's employees huddled in a corner. A man and a woman, both wearing dirty white aprons.

The young cop, an Anglo, was trying to question the male, a young man with close-cropped black hair who kept shaking his head and saying, "*No sé....*"

Out of patience, the cop turned to the woman, an older woman wearing a net over her gray hair. "What about you? Do you work here?"

The woman threw up her arms. "*No hablo Ingles.*"

Fernando thought about offering his services as a translator but lost interest when he saw something out back, something he didn't like. He walked through the kitchen into some sort of addition or lean-to built on the back of the building with its own entrance and exit. In the elongated room he saw two bunk beds and one single bed, along with clothes hampers stacked with an assortment of clothes and toiletries. The single bed and the lower levels of both bunk beds were covered with blankets. It dawned on him that Tryzinski's workers were living in the lean-to. Living in a shack and working for next to nothing, no doubt.

Fernando walked back into the kitchen and confronted Tryzinski.

"So you're housing and exploiting undocumented workers at the same time you're leading an anti-immigration campaign, is that right?"

Tryzinski shot back, "So what? It's just business. At least they're not living on the street!"

Fernando's body tensed. "You're pathetic...you fucking hyprocrite!" He wished the small man would take a swing at him. Just one. That's all the excuse he would need to cover what he wanted to do to Tryzinski.

"Watch it, I'm gonna be on City Council," Tryzinski said.

"Hah! When this story comes out, you'll be lucky if you're not in jail," Fernando said.

Just then they heard screaming outside.

Fernando left Tryzinski and ran out of the lean-to into a back alley. He saw Antonio chasing the runner across an open lot, a young man wearing jeans and a white T-shirt. Manny and the other cop watched from the alley. The runner had a head start, but Antonio caught him just before he reached the next street. The big man tackled the runner from behind and fell on top of him. The runner screamed bloody murder as Antonio twisted his arms and cuffed him from behind.

Manny shouted something to Antonio, who nodded.

Antonio grabbed the runner's belt and lifted him up on his feet and then shoved him toward the restaurant. The two of them came back together, with Antonio shoving the runner from behind to keep him going.

"Good work," Manny said to Antonio. "Thanks."

Fernando got a good look at the runner and saw why he had run. Fingernails had clawed four deep grooves down the left side of his face, from his eye socket all the way down his neck. It wasn't difficult to guess whose fingernails had done the damage. Old Bill had put up a good fight.

The five of them walked back into the restaurant. Manny turned to the young cop. "Sean, you take our friend here in for a statement."

"His name is José," Tryzinski interjected.

"Okay, get a translator to read José his rights and conduct the interrogation. And call Forensics right away to get fingerprints and DNA." Sean nodded.

"Antonio, you drop off Fernando and bring back a translator for the other two workers," Manny continued. "We need to find out who they are and what they're doing here. I'll stay here and get a statement from Trysinzki."

Tryzinski scowled at Manny but said noting.

"Sounds good," Sean said. He pushed José forward and took him out to their cruiser, put him in the rear seat, and drove off down Cerrillos Road.

Fernando followed Antonio outside, leaving Manny with Tryzinski and his two workers.

Once outside, Antonio turned and glared at the flag and the red, white, and blue neon sign on the side of the restaurant. "He doesn't wrap himself in the flag much, does he?"

As an ex-Marine and a veteran of the first Iraq war, Antonio took offense at phony patriotism. He'd come back from his last tour of duty in Iraq suffering from a case of PTSD so severe that it had cost him his marriage. He now lived alone in a mountain cabin near Pecos at the edge of the Santa Fe National Forest. He had a good thirty-mile commute to Santa Fe.

Fernando patted Antonio on the back. "Oldest trick in the book if you want to break the law and get away with it. The refuge of scoundrels."

Antonio frowned and marched to his cruiser.

Once in the cruiser Fernando called Fidel on his cell phone to give him the lead story for the next day's *Independent*: a scoop about Tryzinski and his undocumented workers and their involvement in Old Bill's murder.

Tryzinski could kiss his political career goodbye.

16

After Antonio dropped him off at his office, Fernando took a can of Modelo out of his tiny refrigerator and sat down with his feet on the desk to brood. A black cloud had descended, taking him to the dark place. He didn't like what he'd seen at the restaurant: Tryzinski exploiting his immigrant workers and at the same time campaigning on race and immigrant baiting. The depth of human depravity overwhelmed him, even after thirty-some years in the profession. The thought that Tryzinski's political career would be over as soon as news of his misdeeds went public offered little comfort. The world was full of people like Tryzinski.

To get out of his dark mood Fernando needed to work. That had always been his way of keeping the dark thoughts at bay. Problem was, at the moment he didn't really have a client or a case, just Wayne and this creature with a red face that may or may not be killing homeless people in Santa Fe. How nebulous was that? He cursed Wayne for getting him involved in all this nonsense.

Then Fernando remembered the bloody rags beside an easel in Wayne's house. Wayne couldn't, or at any rate wouldn't, explain the bloody rags. Why?

That got Fernando wondering if there was a connection between Wayne's bloody rags and Ricardo Aragon, the Mexican painter renting the old Forest Service building behind Wayne's house. Wayne may have visited Ricardo, based on his tall tale of being held captive in a nearby shed. Ricardo's wife Maria had gone out of her way to prevent Fernando from seeing Ricardo. Something about Maria seemed suspicious. She wanted to keep Fernando away from her husband. Why?

Then Fernando remembered that Blaine had mentioned meeting Ricardo and agreeing to sell some of Ricardo's paintings in his gallery. Maybe Blaine had more information about Ricardo––like why Ricardo's wife wanted to keep him hidden. Fernando's curiosity got the better of him. He wanted to know more. He needed to know more.

Maybe the black cloud would lift.

So Fernando finished his Modelo, locked the office, and walked down Canyon Road past El Farol to Blaine's gallery, Picasso and Co. Locals joked that it was more Co. than Picasso, but Blaine did well with the tourists who flooded Canyon Road from May through December. While the corporate galleries went for the big bucks, Blaine generally kept his prices reasonable and featured the kind of landscapes, albeit abstract, that tourists tended to like.

Picasso and Co. sat back from Canyon Road a good one hundred feet, with a sidewalk curving through a cactus garden to the front door of the tan adobe with bright blue trim on its windows and door. The side parking lot was empty at the moment.

Fernando walked though the cactus garden and up to the front door. Since the sign on the door said 'Open,' he helped himself. As soon as he stepped inside he saw Blaine arranging bottles of wine and glasses on a long table set up in the rear of the gallery. Blaine wore his usual red Bermuda shorts, with a loud yellow Hawaiian shirt under a blue blazer. Blaine's long black hair fell across his forehead and smothered his ears. True to his reputation as something of a wild man, he rushed back and forth into his office, bringing trays of cheese and meat, hair flying and clothing discombobulated, whatever that meant.

"God-damn, it's hot in here," Blaine said, removing his blazer and tossing it back in his office. Then he noticed Fernando standing by the door. "Fernando, my man! You're early. It doesn't start 'til four o'clock."

"What doesn't start until four?" Fernando asked.

"Oh...shit," Blaine said. "I thought you were here for the reception. I'm giving Ricardo Aragon a reception to kick off the opening of his show, four to six o'clock this afternoon. Should bring in a shit-load of customers, because I put up fliers all over town. Got to take care of business. I guess you know that. Well, maybe not, since you were just a cop all your life and now a private investigator, which is the same damn thing last time I checked. So how you doin'?"

"Same old Blaine," Fernando said. "Are you just naturally higher than a kite, or do you achieve that chemically?"

Blaine laughed. "Both. Which reminds me, now that weed is legal in New Mexico, do you think I should put out a stash of something alongside the cheese and crackers? In case someone wants to imbibe?"

Fernando shrugged. "I don't know, Blaine. My guess is that anyone who shows up at Picasso and Co. will be packing their own weed."

"Hmmm...maybe," Blaine said. "So you're not here for the show."

"No, I just stopped in to take a look at Ricardo's paintings," Fernando said. "I didn't know about the reception."

"Well then, let me give you a tour," Blaine said, and swept the hair out of his eyes. A big man, almost as big as Antonio but not nearly as muscular, Blaine clomped across the wooden floor to the side wall and raised his hands. "*Voila!* What do you think?"

Fernando approached the wall, looking at a smorgasbord of colors: six large and two smaller canvasses that together covered the entire wall. The paintings were abstracted representations of Mexican villages, some in the mountains and others along rivers. The scenes of adobe buildings, carretas and canoes resembled any number of old Spanish villages in northern New Mexico. The colors were transcendent: a vibrant yellow that evoked paradise, a smoky green that suggested life, a nuanced shade of blue that seemed to represent sky, and a flat reddish brown that had a Mother of Pearl finish. Placed side by side, the paintings looked spectacular.

"Wow!" Fernando said.

"See what I mean," Blaine boasted. "This guy's got some mojo!"

"What do you know about him?" Fernando asked.

Blaine looked offended. "What do I need to know? He's from Mexico...he's staying at the old Forest Service building on Upper Canyon Road...and he's offering me twenty percent of the sales price."

"But isn't it strange that he just suddenly appeared out of nowhere, living in an abandoned building?" Fernando asked.

Blaine shrugged. "Could be because he's a blood painter."

"Blood painter?" Fernando asked, jolted by the term.

"Yeah, he paints with blood," Blaine said. "It's a thing. Google it-- look it up. It's popular in Europe and South America. You just add a little blood when you mix your paints. The blood gives the colors a flat, creamy look. Like the reds you see in Ricardo's paintings."

"No kidding," Fernando said, taking a closer look at the paintings. Then he turned back to Blaine. "Where do blood painters get the blood?"

Blaine shrugged. "Depends. If all you need's a couple of drops, you can cut your fingertips. If you need more, you can cut the fleshy part of your underarm. That's what I've been told, anyway. I'm not a painter. I just sell the product."

Fernando considered what Blaine had just said. He nodded once and then kept nodding, not knowing what to say.

"The only other blood painter I knew was a crazy old bastard up in Truchas," Blaine added. "He had his studio in a barn. Used blood from his farm animals, but he created problems by using too much. That's the thing. You can't use too much blood when you mix."

"Why's that?" Fernando asked.

"Starts to stink. Bodily fluids."

Fernando laughed, sort of. "And you say Ricardo will be here today from four to six o'clock?"

"Yeah, man," Blaine said. "I sent out plenty invitations, so the bastard better be here. You should stop by."

"I just might do that," Fernando said.

17

The fact that Ricardo and presumably his wife Maria would be at Blaine's gallery for two hours that afternoon afforded Fernando the opportunity to search their A-frame, inside and out. He just had to kill a long hour. So he took his time walking up Canyon Road to his office. Once there he finished reading the morning *Independent* and tossed the rag into his trash receptacle. Then he did some research on the computer, Googgling the words 'blood painting.' Just as Blaine claimed, the internet took him to dozens of websites dedicated to blood painting. The sites provided information about how to mix blood with paint and how to get blood from your body. He even found videos demonstrating the various procedures. Everything someone interested in blood painting could possibly want to know.

Fernando waited until half past four o'clock before leaving his office. He drove his Cherokee to the end of Canyon Road and found a narrow dirt road leading to the A-frame. Only the tip of the A-frame was visible from Canyon Road, which added to its seclusion at the edge of the Santa Fe National Forest. He saw no other buildings that far into the foothills.

His Cherokee bucked up and down over the rough road as Fernando drove across the sagebrush mesa toward the A-frame. Coming closer he looked for the VW camper van with Chihuahua license plates. He breathed easier when he didn't see the van anywhere. To be safe he drove around behind the A-frame so the Cherokee wouldn't be visible from the road. Just in case he had visitors.

Fernando pulled up beside a large propane tank outside what turned out to be the kitchen window. Before climbing out of the Cherokee, he opened the glove compartment to take out his Smith & Wessen. Then he had second thoughts. If he did encounter someone, Aragon's wife or brother, a weapon might incite an already awkward situation. Better to go unarmed.

He closed the door behind him and surveyed the landscape. Ahead he saw a flat section of a tree stump and a pile of firewood, some of it already split by an axe stuck in the stump. Looked like about a quarter cord of wood, not nearly enough to get the Aragons through the winter, if they were planning to stay that long. Just beyond the woodpile was a fire pit surrounded by three old, rusted metal chairs. Around the corner he saw a gas operated generator. A faint hiking trail wound its way from the rear of the A-frame to the foothills and disappeared into a dark green forest of ponderosa pine. An ideal location, if you wanted seclusion.

Not surprisingly, the rear door was locked tight. He checked the window near the propane tank. Inside he saw a small, efficiency kitchen and a hallway leading into the front rooms. Deserted, as he expected. So he took out his lock pick and went to work on the lock, jimmying it open. When it clicked, he opened the door and stepped into a hot, musty smelling kitchen. He found a brown, discolored propane stove and a small refrigerator sitting idle on the linoleum floor, its door wide open. Replacing the refrigerator were two Igloo coolers stacked on the floor. The lack of windows and fresh air was stifling.

Fernando left the back door open and moved into the hallway, finding two bedrooms, one on each side of the hall. Both bedrooms had an air mattress on the floor and bags of clothing placed on cardboard boxes that substituted as tables. He bypassed the bedrooms and walked into the large front room, which had a sitting area on one side and Ricardo's studio on the other side. A stairway at the end of the hallway led to a partial upper floor.

Fernando decided to check out the loft first, so he climbed up the narrow, rickety stairs made of two-by-six unfinished boards. At the top he entered a square, sunny room with windows on all four sides and not a stick of furniture. Instead, the room was being used for storage. He saw paper and plastic bags from Smith's packed with food items. Further back, placed against the wall, he found a trove of artist supplies: rolls of canvas, tubes and cans of oil paint, several 32 oz. jugs of Turpenoid, and an entire box of bottles of White Spirit Solvent. Looked like Ricardo planned to do some serious painting during his stay.

Not wasting any time, he hurried back downstairs into the front room, where a square folding table, a folding chaise, and several folding chairs were set up in the living area. Mostly camping gear, from what he could tell, along with a Coleman camping stove over in a corner of the room along with several small bottles of propane.

In the studio area on the other side of the room Fernando saw a half painted canvas on an easel by the windows. The painting resembled those he'd seen at Blaine's Picasso and Co. gallery, except this one was a sunset rendering of the same adobe village, with a reddish-purple sky and dark, ominous streets. Not the sunny, quaint, colorful village he'd seen earlier. At sunset the village had a completely different feel. The dark side of the village.

Further down stood a rectangular folding table covered with brown paper. At one end of the table he found a messy scattering of paints and solvents and glass jars, some with brushes soaking in turpentine or other solvents. Two wooden palettes, stained with splotches of paint, lay in the center of the table. What interested him most were the stainless steel trays and instruments at the far end of the table, next to a nearby wooden chair. Inside the largest tray, a covered instrument tray, he found several medical lances and scalpels. Other flat trays held gauze pads and bandages of different sizes, as well as bottles of rubbing alcohol.

Then Fernando spotted what he was looking for: kidney-shaped trays with splotches of paint and dried blood inside the rims. The one-inch deep trays had been used as palettes. Standing there, Fernando imagined Ricardo slicing the soft underside of his arm and bleeding into the tray and then mixing his blood with paint. Made him cringe to think about it. Painting with your own blood seemed like such a crazy thing to do. What did it add to the painting?

Suddenly he heard a noise outside the A-frame very close to the front door. A humming noise: "Mmmmm...." The same humming noise he'd heard in the trees along the Santa Fe River before he encountered the creature with the red face. He was sure it was the same sound.

What to do? He looked around for a place to hide, even though since his Cherokee was parked out back, the creature would soon know he was here. If it didn't already know.

Once again Fernando berated himself for not bringing his Smith & Wessen. What had he been thinking?

With no good options, he crept into the hall and hid on the first step of the stairway. He heard the humming sound again, getting louder. The creature was approaching the front door of the A-frame. That gave him a chance.

As soon as he heard a key fumbling in the lock, Fernando bolted. He ran to the kitchen and outside to the Cherokee. He slammed the door and started the engine. Throwing the gearshift into reverse, he spun the big vehicle backwards onto the open mesa. Then he shifted into drive and took off fast, spinning his tires in the soft sand. He swerved back onto the dirt road and lurched forward, leaving a billowing plume of dust behind.

Not wearing a seatbelt, he bounced up and down in the car seat as he careened down the winding road. Halfway to Canyon Road he glanced in the rearview mirror. He didn't see anything behind him, only a dark cloud of dust following him like the Grim Reaper himself.

18

Fernando braked and brought the Cherokee to a stop when he reached Canyon Road. He looked again in his rearview mirror, still paranoid even though he'd seen no other vehicles at the A-frame. The coast was clear, so he pulled out on Canyon Road and drove slowly into the city. He decided to stop at Wayne's adobe rather than go directly to Blaine's gallery for the reception, just to check on Wayne. He turned into the familiar alley and drove up the hill to Wayne's house.

By the time he parked and climbed out of the Cherokee, Wayne was standing in front of his adobe. The old man's hair seemed even whiter than the last time Fernando had seen him. Maybe the hospital stay had aged Wayne. Dealing with doctors and nurses could have that effect, as Fernando knew from his own experience. Too many visits to the Emergency Room.

Today Wayne wore the clothes given to him by the hospital: khakis and a plaid flannel shirt under a dirty white apron smudged with paint. Fernando laughed when he saw this, not used to seeing Wayne in anything but his ancient black suit.

"What are you laughing at, Lopez?" Wayne asked, coming out to meet him.

"You, that's what," Fernando said. "You look almost...I don't know... contemporary."

"Hah!" Wayne replied. "So what do you want? What are you doing here?"

Fernando noticed the towel in Wayne's hands, one of the blood-stained towels he'd seen earlier. "Just checking on you––like the docs at the hospital asked me to. What, are you doing more blood painting?"

Wayne looked confused. "Blood painting? What the hell's that?"

"You mix your blood with the paint," Fernando said. "Like you were doing before, remember? The test tube? The bloody towels?"

Wayne raised his bloody towel and studied it. "What?"

"Don't you remember?" Fernando asked. "You walked up to the old

Forest Service building where Ricardo Aragon is painting with blood. You must have gotten some tips from him, because you came back and tried it here. That's where the bloody towels came from."

Wayne looked confused. "Who's Richard Aragon? I don't remember any of that. I don't know what the hell you're talking about. I just cut myself or something, I don't know."

Fernando frowned. "Whatever you say. So you're getting along okay? You need anything?"

Wayne shook his head. "Why the hell wouldn't I be okay?"

Fernando raised his voice. "You just got out of the hospital, Wayne! I'm just checking up on you!"

"I did? News to me," Wayne said.

"You don't remember the hospital? They gave you the clothes you're wearing."

Wayne, confused, looked down at his clothes and then turned and walked back into his adobe.

Fernando considered following Wayne and showing him his hospital discharge papers, which Fernando had placed in a letter holder on his kitchen counter, but then decided the hell with it. Why bother?

It was clear to Fernando that Wayne was losing his grip on reality. The old man needed help badly. They would have to do some kind of intervention, Ruby and Blaine and whoever else he could enlist. Soon.

Giving up, Fernando climbed back in his Cherokee and checked his watch: forty minutes past five o'clock. That gave him twenty minutes. He drove back to Canyon Road and down to the Picasso and Co. gallery. He wanted to meet Ricardo Aragon. He had questions that needed answers. Namely, who was this creature with the red face who walked around humming.

The parking lot next to Picasso and Co. was half-full when Fernando arrived. He parked, set the brake, and walked into the gallery. At this late hour most of the attendees had congregated by the refreshment table, where Blaine held court. Wearing his blue blazer over red Bermuda shorts, Blaine towered over everyone else at the table. His voice boomed: "So when I first saw one of Ricardo's paintings, I said, 'GODDAMN, that looks like a J. M.W. Turner with BALLS. I mean, look at those deep colors. And the creamy overlay. You can't get that with anything but blood. When he asked if I would take a couple for the gallery, I said HELL yes. I'll do better'n that--I'll give you a show."

Fernando saw Ricardo up front talking to a blowsy blonde wearing a straw hat, gray vest, tight black stretch pants, and an armful of silver bracelets. Ricardo, on the other hand, was a model of understatement. Wearing a black Mexican Guayabera shirt over jeans, Ricardo had a quiet, unpretentious demeanor. He spoke softly and listened earnestly to the blonde, nodding his classically handsome face with aquiline nose and raven black hair. Slender and buff, he looked to be in his mid to late forties. A real looker.

But something else caught Fernando's attention. Ricardo was missing a little finger on his right hand. Instead of a finger, there was a stub about as big as a thimble. Some sort of accident had taken his little finger.

Ricardo seemed to be in an intense discussion with the blonde, so Fernando headed for the refreshment table. Maria Aragon sat off to the side of the table, holding a drink in her hand and looking uncomfortable. She wore a tight black dress and silver jewelry that perfectly complemented her black hair. He approached slowly, trying to put the woman at ease. She smiled tentatively when she saw him coming. She seemed nervous, always looking around as if on the lookout for bad luck or bad people who would harm her.

"Mr. Lopez," Maria said, and held out her hand.

Fernando shook her hand. "How's the reception going?"

"Good...I think," she said. "I just watch, but I think Ricardo sell one, maybe two paintings already."

Fernando nodded. "I can see why. The paintings are striking, very unusual."

Maria smiled, but not convincingly. She looked worried.

Fernando glanced around the room and then turned back to Maria. "Where's Ricardo's brother? Didn't you say Ricardo had a brother staying with you?"

Maria winced. "*Si, el no esta bien.* He stay behind."

"Sorry to hear that. What's his problem?" Fernando asked.

Maria looked down and whispered so only he could hear, "*No puedo hablar.* No can talk here."

Again Fernando looked around the room. No one was paying any attention to them. He handed Maria another of his cards and said, "Here's another card. "Call me when you can talk. Or if you need help. Understand?"

Maria nodded.

Then Fernando made his way to the far end of the table and grabbed a plastic glass of champagne just to be social. He rarely drank anything stronger than beer. The champagne tasted about as cheap as the plastic glass. Still, he shot down the champagne and tossed the plastic glass in a nearby trash receptacle.

When the blowsy blonde abandoned Ricardo, Fernando walked over and introduced himself to Ricardo. "I'm a friend of Wayne Fontenot, a painter who I think you know."

Ricardo nodded. "Yes, he stop by our house the other day. I show him my work. He say he interested in blood painting, so I show him how. I give him a test tube filled with blood to start."

Fernando had to hand it to Ricardo. The man was calm, cool, and collected.

"He seem, I dunno, a little confused," Ricardo added.

Fernando laughed. "Confused is a good word for it. He suffers from mild to moderate dementia."

"I see," Ricardo said.

"So tell me, where do you get your blood?" Fernando asked abruptly.

Ricardo was clearly taken aback. He frowned. "Blood letting, how do you think?" He raised his arm to show the scars in the soft underside of the arm

"You don't harvest blood from strangers?" Fernando asked quickly, before Ricardo could walk away. "You and your brother?"

"No, of course not," Ricardo said. "That would be illegal."

"Yes, it would," Fernando said as Ricardo hurried over to join Maria.

Fernando watched the two of them hurry out of the gallery, with Ricardo squeezing her arm so tight it made Maria cry out. Ricardo slammed the door behind them.

Fernando rushed to the window and watched them drive away in their VW camper van. It looked like Maria was weeping in the front passenger seat.

19

Fernando was a few minutes late for their twice-monthly Friday afternoon Happy Hour at La Fonda Bar. He and Antonio and Fidel met for drinks at La Fonda every other Friday. Sometimes Manny joined them, and once in a great while another of the *Independent* reporters showed up with Fidel, but that was rare given the cutbacks at the *Independent*. Today he saw only Antonio and Fidel as he walked though the carved wooden doors of the La Fonda Hotel.

Fernando loved La Fonda, the historic hotel on the Plaza that all the new designer hotels in Santa Fe tried, and failed, to emulate. A Harvey Hotel back in the nineteen twenties, La Fonda was chock full of Southwestern arts and crafts, from Pueblo pottery and Navajo rugs in glass cases to historic paintings and murals on the walls. If Estelle ever kicked him out of the house, he would go directly to La Fonda. Or so he told himself.

Antonio waved from one of the rear tables, just in case he hadn't noticed them. Fernando waved back and then wound his way through the crowded bar and took a seat at the table.

"You're late," Antonio said.

"Yeah, I've been running around town, trying to catch up," Fernando said, out of breath. "I was hoping Manny would be here. I have some news about the creature with the red face."

Antonio checked his watch. "Manny said he didn't know if he could make it today."

Fidel waited until Fernando sat down and then said, "I was just telling Antonio about the story I filed for tomorrow's paper. Turns out Tryzinski was booked on charges of hiring and harboring undocumented immigrants. Booked and released, of course. He's being represented by none other than Raoul Garcia."

"How the screw turns," Fernando said, shaking his head. Raoul

Garcia was the best criminal lawyer in the state of New Mexico. His nickname was 'Guilty Man Walking' because he managed to get even the guiltiest of clients off scot-free. He and Raoul were old combatants. Raoul always won.

"That doesn't make any sense," Fernando said. "Raoul's an old Lefty, he made his reputation by defending hippies and radicals. Tryzinski is a Right Wing fanatic. How can Raoul defend him?"

Fidel laughed. "Haven't you heard, money has replaced politics. For Raoul and everybody else."

Fernando waved at the bartender, an old timer with a handlebar mustache and a twinkle in his eye whose name was Phil. "Hey, partner, what can I get you?" Phil asked, coming around the bar. "Your usual?"

"Yep, Modelo draft," Fernando said.

"You got it," Phil said and ambled back to the bar.

Fernando turned to Antonio and Fidel. "What about José, the guy with scratches down his face that you arrested?"

"He was booked and jailed for first degree murder," Antonio said. "Not only that, but José had a crisp one hundred dollar bill in his pants--just like we found on the other undocumented worker who died after raiding Bill's camp."

"No kidding," Fernando said.

Antonio nodded. "Forensics found Tryzinski's fingerprints on the hundred dollar bill in possession of the dead guy. They expect to find it on the bill José had. If they do, Tryzinski will be facing charges a lot more serious than hiring and harboring undocumented immigrants."

"He's not very bright," Fidel said. "He's just a thug."

Everyone agreed with that diagnosis.

"Well, here's my news," Fernando said. "I think our vampire killer is none other than the brother of Ricardo Aragon, the Mexican painter whose work Blaine is showing at Picasso and Co."

Fernando recounted his two encounters with the red-faced creature, the first along the Santa Fe River and the second at the old Forest Service building on Upper Canyon Road that Richard Aragon and his wife Maria were renting.

Fidel looked doubtful. "You're saying Richard Aragon's brother is the vampire killer?"

Fernando nodded. "Yeah, but he's not a vampire. I'm not even sure he's a killer."

"What do you mean? You saw the bodies, or at least one of the bodies," Antonio said.

Fernando told them about his conversation with Maria Aragon. "She said Ricardo's brother wasn't well, but didn't explain. She couldn't really talk. I'll try to contact her tomorrow."

"Good, because I don't have probable cause to go poking around up there," Antonio said.

"Since when do you guys need probable cause?" Fidel asked.

Antonio shot him a dirty look.

"Here's the thing," Fernando said. "Ricardo does blood painting. To do that he needs blood. He told me uses his own blood. He even showed me the scars on his arm where he cut himself. The question is: does he need more blood than he can supply himself."

Just then they spotted Manny coming in the front door of La Fonda. Manny came into the bar and danced through the tables, a wise-ass grin on his baby face. "Afternoon, ladies, can I join you for a lemonade?"

Manny sat next to Antonio, who was a foot taller than the little man with the youthful face. No matter what the occasion, Manny was always in a good mood. Today was no exception.

"Better late than never," Fernando said.

"You guys look like you've just come from a funeral," Manny said. "What's up?"

Fidel brought Manny up to speed on their conversation thus far.

Manny smiled. "Well, I hate to bring you more bad news, but I've just come from another homicide scene. This one's way up at the end of Camino Cabre, right where it connects with Arroyo de los Chamisos."

"Where the hell is that?" Antonio asked.

"It's south off Upper Canyon Road," Manny said. "In the middle of nowhere."

"Never heard of it," Fernando added.

"You will now, *amigo*," Manny responded. "We got a white male, by the name of Billy Johnson, age 23, with his throat cut and a bullet in the back of his head. His car was pushed into the arroyo with all its windows smashed out. A guy out for a morning walk with his dog found him this morning. How's that for a way to start your day?"

Fernando shifted in his chair. "You say his throat was cut?"

Manny nodded. "Not only that, but whoever killed him tortured him first and then shot him in the head execution style. Both of his ears were removed and two of his fingers were chopped off at the knuckle. Quite a sight. A real butcher, whoever did this."

"Jesus!" Fidel said. "Does the news desk know?"

Manny smiled. "You do now."

"What do you have so far?" Fernando asked.

"Nothing good," Manny said. "Thing is, we found the remains of fentanyl in the trashed car. Bags, plastic wrap, the works. The guy was trafficking fentanyl for the cartel."

"The Sinaloa Cartel," Antonio added.

"Right," Manny said. "They control the flow of drugs into New Mexico and then east through Texas. They have a big operation in Albuquerque's Barelas neighborhood. From Albuquerque they're moving it up I-25 to Santa Fe. Lots of money in Santa Fe, which means lots of drugs. You know how it works."

Fidel stood up and waved at the bartender. "Another round, Phil."

Phil saluted from the bar.

"We think the dead guy must have double-crossed his handler, maybe siphoned off a little too much of the profit and lied about it," Manny continued. "And the cartel does what it always does: a little torture followed by a bullet to the back of the head."

Antonio nodded. "That's the signature of Silva Archivada, who replaced Chapo."

Fernando was curious. "These other homicides involving homeless people...could they have been the work of Archivada?"

"Not the one under the Delgado Street Bridge," Manny said. "I don't know about the other one. It's possible."

Fernando didn't like what he'd just heard. He didn't know which was worse, a vampire killer or a Mexican drug cartel, but he suspected the latter.

20

Saturday morning broke wild and windy, with massive cirrus clouds blowing in over the Sangre de Cristo Mountains East of Santa Fe. Fernando took his second cup of coffee into his studio and booted up his computer planning to research the Sinaloa Cartel. He'd been under the impression, or at least he had hoped, that the Mexican drug cartels would spread out along the major interstates that bisected the state, I-25 north and south and both I-40 and I-10 east and west, and leave the smaller communities in Northern New Mexico alone. If what Manny said was true, that wasn't the case. Santa Fe might be small, but it had become the playground of the rich and famous. Drugs followed money like night followed day, just as Manny said.

Fernando's search turned up several news stories about the Sinaloa Cartel from newspapers in Albuquerque, Las Cruces, and El Paso, Texas. He paid more attention to the Albuquerque stories, since Albuquerque was a mere sixty miles south of Santa Fe. He found several recent stories about a Sinaloa crime wave in the Albuquerque newspapers: shootings on the West Mesa, brutal murders in the South Valley, and the growing Sinaloa presence in Albuquerque's Barelas neighborhood. Most of them mentioned Silva Archivada as the head of the cartel. So it was true. Sinaloa was moving north and Santa Fe would not be spared. That was the takeaway.

While he sat in front of his computer considering what he'd just read, he heard Estelle close the kitchen door on her way to the Immigrant Outreach Program downtown. He switched off his computer and walked into the kitchen to make himself an early lunch, a turkey sandwich and a handful of potato chips. By the time he finished eating it was half past eleven. Time to head to the office.

Fernando drove down Acequia Madre to the Paseo and around to Canyon Road, dodging pedestrian tourists as he made his way up to his office. Santa Fe was crawling with end-of-summer tourists trying desperately to find a moment's pleasure before the drudgery of school and work began for another year. He parked his Cherokee next to Ruby's Honda and followed the twisting gravel path to his office. Coming closer, he spotted a note taped to the glass on his door with Ruby's effusively scribbled signature at the bottom. The note read:

"Fernando, a woman came by the gallery this morning looking for you. She thought your office might be part of my gallery (go figure!). She wouldn't leave her name. Watch out for this one. She's hot!"

He tore off the note and carried it inside his office. He had no idea who the woman was, unless Crystal had stopped by to tell him she'd seen the creature with the red face again. Whoever it was, she hadn't left a message on his machine.

He barely had time to sit at his desk before he heard gravel crunching outside. Moments later he saw a shadow falling across the window in the door. Then a knock on the door.

"Come in!" he shouted a little too loudly, not used to people knocking. They usually walked right in and unloaded their troubles. On him.

The door opened and Maria Aragon walked tentatively into his office, as nervous as ever.

Fernando saw immediately what Ruby had meant. Maria looked like a million bucks, wearing tight jeans and a silk shirt tied in front that exposed her midsection. Her ruffled black hair fell playfully across her round face, accented by a pair of Sarah Palin glasses that made her look incredibly sexy.

"Mr. Lopez, you gave me your card," Maria said, and held up one of the cards he'd given her.

"Yes, two of them, in fact," he said awkwardly.

Maria blushed. "I thought...well, do you have a few minutes?"

"Of course. Come sit down," Fernando said.

Maria walked carefully to the chair and sat, hands in her lap, looking down at the floor.

"What's up?" he asked, a little too cavalierly, he realized after the fact.

Maria burst into tears. She buried her head in her hands.

Feeling responsible for her tears, Fernando said, "I'm so sorry if I upset you. Please. Tell me how I can help. What can I do for you?"

Maria reached across his desk and took a tissue from the box he kept on his desk for just these situations. She dried her eyes and said, "I'm very stressed right now, I'm sorry."

"Don't be," Fernando said. "I'd like to help, if I can."

"See, we are hiding out here, me and Ricardo and his brother Oscar," Maria explained. "My husband is a painter, you know. He belongs to the *Los Pintores Sangre* group in Juarez. His brother Oscar was a policeman who made a big mistake. He took bribes from the cartel and then they forced him to carry drugs for them."

"*Cartel de Sinaloa?*" he asked.

"*Si,*" she said, nodding. "When Oscar tried to stop the drugs they shot him in the head." She pointed to the side of her head. "The bullet damaged his brain, not kill him. That is why he is the way he is."

"What way is that?" Fernando asked. "You're talking about the guy with the red face who goes around humming, right?"

Maria nodded. "He no longer can talk now, only hum."

"Does he help Ricardo obtain blood?" Fernando asked.

She looked down again and didn't speak for several seconds. When she did it was with a sigh. "He offers his own blood, from the arm. And twice now, once in Albuquerque and once right here, he tried to take it from someone else."

"Killed someone to get their blood, you mean?" Fernando asked.

Tears streamed down Maria's face. "I think so. He came back with a container of blood. Lot of blood."

Fernando watched Maria closely. She seemed genuine. That is, she seemed to be telling the truth. "Is that why you left Albuquerque and came to Santa Fe?"

"Yes, and because the cartel found us in Albuquerque," Maria said. "They cut off one of Ricardo's fingers and threatened to kill him. They want him to carry drugs from Juarez into U.S. because he travels back and forth selling his paintings. If Ricardo refuses, they say they will kill all of us, one at a time. Maybe me first, or maybe Oscar."

"Okay, I understand, you're running from the cartel, but do they know where you're living now?" Fernando asked.

Maria nodded, tears forming in her eyes again.

"How did they find you?"

"They saw the notice Mister Blaine put in the newspaper about Ricardo's reception," Maria said. "They found out from him where we live and came to see us on the mountain."

"Were they driving a silver Toyota?" Fernando asked. "A 4Runner?"

"Yes, a Toyota."

Good old Blaine, Fernando thought. He still had bad memories of Blaine fucking up Jimmy Mackey's life. Looked like Blaine was doing it again.

"How many of them were there?" Fernando asked.

"Two, one big guy and one small guy who does the talking," Maria said. "The big guy was the one who cut Ricardo's finger. Very dangerous."

Fernando laughed, in spite of himself. "I'd say so."

"Can you help us?"

Fernando took a deep breath. This was not something he wanted to get involved in. "Have you talked to the Santa Fe Police? I can introduce you to the lead detective and a sergeant who's good at dealing with these kinds of people."

"No, no police," Maria said. "Ricardo refuses to go to the police because of his involvement with the cartel earlier."

The more he heard, the less Fernando liked the situation. "Thing is, these cartel guys are like rats or cockroaches—if you see one, there's dozens more. Maybe hundreds."

Maria sat in silence, her hands in her lap. She nodded and then looked around the room before coming back to Fernando.

Fernando waited. The ball was in her court.

She sighed. "We can't keep running, because whenever Ricardo sells a painting or has a show they can find us."

Fernando nodded. "I understand. That's why the police might be able to help, get you far away from the border."

"No, you don't understand, the Sinaloa Cartel is everywhere, all the major cities on East and West coasts. Even cities like Denver and Chicago and others in Midwest."

Fernando's cell phone rang, interrupting their conversation. He reached over and clicked off the call.

"We can pay you," Maria continued.

Fernando laughed. "For what? What do you want me to do?"

"Can you protect us?" she asked.

"From the cartel?" he asked, flabbergasted. "How do you expect me to do that?"

Maria shook her head. "I don't know...I don't know what to do."

Fernando considered. He didn't like the look of disappointment on her face. He had always been a sucker for the woman in distress sort of thing. Always against his better judgment.

"Okay," he said, tapping the top of his desk with his fingers. "Let's do this. Give me a call if they approach you again. My cell phone number is on my card. In the meantime I'll give it some thought. I might be able to round up a posse, so to speak. I can try at any rate."

Maria smiled faintly. She came around the desk and kissed him on the cheek and then walked out of his office.

21

After Maria left his office Fernando called Manny at the Washington Avenue Station. He told Manny about his conversation with Maria and that the Sinaloa Cartel had the Aragon family in its sights. He added that Maria alluded to the possibility that Ricardo's brother Oscar was––or might be––the creature with the red face responsible for the murder of Mike Carter. He made sure to qualify this last statement. Oscar would have to be interviewed and given a chance to respond. That, in itself, could be difficult, because they would have to find someone, Maria or Ricardo probably, who could facilitate communication with Oscar after his head wound left him unable to speak.

"No shit?" Manny said. "I haven't had the pleasure of meeting any of the Aragons, but I guess I will as soon as I can get to it. That's on the back burner at the moment, with the Sinaloa crowd moving into the city. Forensics finished their work at the crime scene on Camino Cabre, the execution style killing. We have reports from two neighbors who claim to have seen a silver Toyota 4Runner in the area that night but no other leads so far. One of the neighbors said the 4Runner had El Paso, Texas license plates.

"What did you find out about the victim?" Fernando asked.

"Billy Johnson? He's just a two-bit crook from Albuquerque who got involved with the wrong crowd, way over his head. He has a record as long as my arm, mostly theft, breaking and entering, and assault with a deadly weapon, your usual run-of-the-mill Albuquerque punk."

Fernando laughed. "The usual, you say?"

They grow a lot of them down there," Manny said and then got serious. "So why did Maria Aragon come to you and not the police?"

"She's afraid to involve the police because of Ricardo and Oscar's involvement with the cartel early on, under duress," Fernando said.

"Hmmm...so what does she want from you?" Manny asked.

"Protection from the cartel?"

"Something like that."

"From the cartel?" Manny asked again. "She doesn't want much, does she?"

"Thanks, I knew I could count on you?" Fernando said and clicked off before Manny could respond with another wisecrack.

In truth, Fernando's take on the situation differed little from Manny's. Protecting someone from a cartel was not a one-person job. It was time to call in the cavalry, except in this case there wasn't any cavalry to call in. Only Manny and Antonio, if they happened to be available when he needed them. A big if.

Fernando brooded for hours on what he could do should Maria call for assistance. He helped himself to an early Modelo and then went next door to tell Ruby about his quandary. Ruby was not sympathetic.

"You know what your problem is, Fernando?" Ruby asked finally. "You're a sucker for the babes. I'm surprised you've always been monogamous. You must be the only one on Canyon Road!"

Fernando laughed. "Well, almost always."

"One weekend in Juarez doesn't count," Ruby said. "I know your history."

It was true. His only indiscretion in more than thirty years of marriage was a weekend in Juarez with Linda Stephens, the Police Dispatcher at the Washington Avenue Station. They'd broken off the affair to save their friendship and his marriage. Estelle forgave him once, but she made it clear she wouldn't do it again. Ever.

While Ruby rattled off a laundry list of her ex husbands and listed the flaws of each and every one of them, Fernando drifted into boredom. Finally he excused himself. He needed to do something. That was the only way to stop his brooding.

He decided to check on Wayne. To make sure Wayne hadn't had any more medical incidents. So he climbed into his Cherokee and drove up Canyon Road. He had to wait at the entrance to the alley leading to Wayne's house while a garbage truck picked up trash in the alley. Then he drove up the hill to Wayne's adobe. He saw no sign of Wayne out front, but when he walked to the adobe and raised his hand to knock on the door, the door suddenly swung open. Wayne stood inside dressed once again in his black suit, which looked almost clean. Cleaner than Fernando had ever seen it, at any rate.

"Damn, Wayne, you look like you're going out on the town,"

Fernando said.

Wayne smiled. "Yessir, I took my suit to the dry cleaner. I'm going out to Claude's tonight. It's Saturday, you know, the night she usually sings cabaret. I think she's sweet on me," he said, beaming.

"Un-huh," Fernando said, debating whether to remind Wayne once again that Claude had been dead for forty years. He decided to keep silent. What's the point? The old geezer would believe what he wanted to believe. Like the rest of us.

"I been cleaning," Wayne said, holding the door open for Fernando. "In case she wants to come back here."

Fernando followed Wayne inside. He smiled when he saw the cleaning Wayne had done. The old man had cleared everything off his two stuffed chairs and picked up the newspapers and magazines on the floor and tossed them in a corner of the front room. That was the extent of Wayne's cleaning.

Suddenly Wayne stopped and looked at him suspiciously, an abrupt Jekyll and Hyde moment. "So why are you here?"

"I wanted to ask if you've seen a silver Toyota 4Runner up here the last day or so," Fernando said.

"Hell yes, I saw it," Wayne said, a little prickly now. "They stopped in here looking for Ricardo Aragon. Two men, one was a big sonofabitch and the other one did all the talking. I didn't appreciate their attitude. They liked to kick in my door when they knocked."

"What did you tell them?" Fernando asked.

"I pointed up to the old Forest Service building and told them to leave me the hell alone," Wayne said. "They left and didn't come back. Good thing. I didn't like the look of the big one. He looked like a thug. Or worse, a killer."

"You're right," Fernando said. "They're dangerous. They belong to the Sinaloa Cartel. Stay away from them."

"I'm trying to, goddammit!"

Fernando looked around the room. "You want some help cleaning? I can give you a hand."

"Yeah, okay, but don't mess up anything," Wayne said. "I got everything in its right place."

So Fernando helped Wayne clean. They swept the floors, made the bed, washed the dirty dishes and the kitchen counters and took piles of trash outside and tossed everything in a mound to burn later. By the time they finished it was show-time at Claude's, according to Wayne. The old man went into the bathroom to wash his face and comb his white hair.

Wayne was smiling when he came out of the bathroom. "I'm ready."

"Okay, let me give you a ride," Fernando said. He led Wayne to the Cherokee and told him to fasten the seat belt.

"I hate those damn things," the old man said.

"I know, but you have to fasten it or the damn thing keeps beeping."

Once Wayne's seat belt was fastened, they drove to the end of the alley and down Canyon Road to the parking lot across from El Farol.

Fernando pulled into the parking lot and turned off the engine. He looked at Wayne. "Here you are."

"Aren't you coming in?" Wayne asked.

"Okay."

The two of them crossed Canyon Road and walked into El Farol, where the regulars were sitting at a back table. Together Ruby and Blaine shouted, "Wayne!"

Wayne smiled and went to join them.

22

Sunday morning Fernando slept in while Estelle went to Mass at Saint Francis Cathedral downtown. He decided to kick back and take it easy for a day, skipping his usual Sunday afternoon at the office. Instead, maybe he would drive out to the village of Pecos and go fishing with Antonio. They hadn't fished together since early spring, when they'd hiked up into the Pecos Wilderness with their fishing equipment. Which was his bad, because Antonio was always ready to go fishing, living as he did in a cabin at the edge of the Santa Fe National Forest. Why not take the day off? He had no actual clients, only people like Wayne and Maria who wanted him to do favors for them *pro bono*. The hell with it, he was going fishing.

The ringing of his cell phone ended his ruminations. He reached across the nightstand and grabbed his phone. His spirits sank when he saw Manny's name and number on the screen. For a moment he considered not answering, but loyalty to his former colleague got the better of him. "Manny, what's up?"

"Hah! Come down to the Delgado Street Bridge and I'll show you what's up. Literally," Manny said.

"What do you mean?" Fernando asked.

"The Sinaloa boys were on the prowl last night," Manny said. "Come on down and I'll show you their work. It's hard to describe, you have to actually see it for yourself."

Fernando winced. There goes his day off. And his fishing trip. "Okay, I'll be right down."

Fernando showered and dressed quickly. Then he drank a cup of coffee and ate a banana. When he finished, he poured another cup of coffee in his stainless steel travel mug and walked outside to his Cherokee. The day was clear and sunny, not a cloud in the sky. Perfect for fishing. Maybe he could take a quick look at whatever Manny wanted to show him and then call Antonio in Pecos. They would still have most of the day to fish along the Pecos River.

So hoping for the best he drove around the Paseo and turned right onto Alameda. One long block east on Alameda took him to Delgado Street. He drove past the bridge and parked illegally behind the ambulance and the police cruisers lining Alameda. He didn't see it until he climbed out of his Cherokee and started walking on the sidewalk toward the bridge. Halfway there he saw what Manny was alluding to. What's up turned out to be a body hanging by its feet from the Delgado Street Bridge.

"Shit!" Fernando cursed out loud. Cancel the fishing trip.

Manny and the others stood on the banks of the Santa Fe River while a police photographer shot photos of the gruesome scene. Teresa from Forensics was combing the area, looking for evidence. Manny stood off to the side with another officer who Fernando didn't recognize. Another new cop who'd been hired in the two years since he'd retired.

It was only when he started to climb down the riverbank that he saw the full horror of the scene ahead. A naked man hung upside down from the bridge, his feet bound with heavy rope tied to the bridge railing. A knife or some other sharp object had sliced him open from his groin down to his chest bone, allowing his intestines to partially fall out of the abdominal cavity. The man's head and shoulders were covered with blood, as was the ground underneath. The white, bloodless corpse moved ever so slightly in the gentle breeze, swinging one way and then the other.

The smell was just as bad as the sight, Fernando realized as he approached. Manny and Teresa both wore masks. The new cop held a handkerchief over his nose. Fernando did the same, pulling a handkerchief out of his rear pocket and holding it over his face. Manny waved from under the bridge, standing off to the side of the hanging corpse.

He stopped about ten yards away from the gruesome object, not wanting to disturb any evidence Teresa might find. Best to keep his distance and let the team do their work. It looked to Fernando like they had just started the investigation.

Manny came right over and lowered his mask. "So there's your Devil on Canyon Road. One of them anyway."

"What do you mean?" Fernando said, not understanding.

"Follow me," Manny said and led the way to the bridge. He motioned toward the dead man. "They shot him in the back of the head and then strung him up and slit him open."

Fernando looked at the misshapen head of Oscar Aragon, trying to avoid the abdominal area. The large, round head had a massive sunken or conclave area on its left side, where a cartel bullet had left an old wound back in Juarez, according to Maria Aragon. The skull had been surgically repaired, but a dent remained. With eyes and mouth wide open, the face was partially covered by blood that had flowed down from the sliced abdomen.

Manny pointed to Oscar's face. "You can see the redness, even where there's no blood. He had a skin condition called rosacea that turns the face red. In warm weather his sweat would turn the skin bright red. So there's your creature with the red face. There's the Devil on Canyon Road."

"One of them," Fernando said.

Manny turned to Fernando.

"That's Oscar Aragon, who I told you about," Fernando said. "He's the brother of Ricardo Aragon, the painter who's living at the old Forest Service building on Upper Canyon Road. Ricardo's the painter Blaine's been talking about, the one who does the blood paintings."

Manny took out his pocket notebook and started writing. "I remember now. Do these people have visas?"

Fernando shrugged. "I don't know. Don't ask, don't tell, that's always been my philosophy. As you know."

Manny nodded.

"Like I said, Ricardo's wife Maria came to see me yesterday and told me the cartel had found where they were staying and threatened them," Fernando continued. "Two men, driving a silver Toyota 4Runner, like the one neighbors saw on Camino Cabre where Billy Johnson was murdered."

"Okay, I'll pay the Aragons a visit after I finish here," Manny said. "I'll need their descriptions of the two thugs in the 4Runner. They'll have to make arrangements for the body of the brother. Whatever Oscar did or didn't do, we'll just have to let slide. Like you say, don't ask, don't tell. You can't charge a dead man. That's a fact."

Fernando agreed. "Take Antonio with you, just in case the two Sinaloa boys make an appearance."

"Oh, yeah, I'll bring Antonio and maybe old Hank Dixon and his 308 Winchester, if I can wake him up."

Fernando laughed. A member of the SFPD Swat Team and a registered sharpshooter, Old Hank was getting long in the tooth. There hadn't been much use for a sharpshooter in recent years. That might be changing now that the cartel had arrived in Santa Fe.

"We may be getting help soon," Manny said. "The Chief called the Feds yesterday afternoon and talked to the DEA office in Albuquerque.

We're supposed to be getting a couple of agents this week. 'Supposed to' is the operative word. You know how that goes."

Fernando frowned. Yes, he did know.

"I just hope it's not too late," Manny said.

Exactly what Fernando was thinking.

23

Fernando didn't leave the Delgado Street Bridge until the ambulance left with Oscar Aragon's body. He followed the ambulance down Alameda, where the ambulance turned left and headed for the morgue at Christus Saint Vincent Hospital on Saint Michael's Drive. He turned right and then left on Palace and continued on down to the Santa Fe Plaza, turning right on Washington Avenue. He took the first parking place he saw on Washington. Since it was well past Noon, he headed for the Great Burrito Company for a quick lunch and more coffee.

He walked down Washington, past the station where he'd worked for thirty years, feeling a twinge of nostalgia. His nostalgia quickly passed as soon as he remembered his longstanding friction with Chief Stuart. He was damn happy to be retired and not have to take orders from that arrogant, irascible sonofabitch. The Chief and the Mayor might have considered him a malcontent, but he wasn't the only one at the Washington Street Station who felt that way about Stuart.

All the employees who worked at the Great Burrito Company knew him by now. Today Eddie and Mary greeted him as he walked through the door. Eddie waved. Mary said, "Coffee, extra cream and sugar!" All three of them laughed.

Mary checked her watch. "You're late today. You must want lunch." A tall, big-boned woman, Mary had some sort of scarf or headdress wrapped around her head that he could not identify or name. She wore her usual uniform, gray shirt embroidered with the burrito logo.

How about brunch? Give me the breakfast burrito, large," Fernando said.

Eddie, AKA Eduardo, quickly assembled the burrito while Fernando stood at the counter. Eddie was a tiny immigrant from Honduras with neat, close-cropped hair and a big smile.

"Thanks, Eddie," Fernando said and took the burrito and coffee outside to a table. He ignored the other people on the patio, not interested in making small talk with the largely tourist crowd. One of his shortcomings, according to Estelle. He could come off as aloof, if not downright unfriendly. So be it. He never claimed to be a social butterfly. Just didn't give a damn.

Church bells rang up the street, reminding him that it was a sleepy Sunday. He took his time eating his burrito and drinking his precious coffee. These days he could never seem to get enough coffee.

Eventually he got bored with the patio scene and left. He walked down Washington to his Cherokee and drove back around to Canyon Road. Ruby closed her gallery on Sundays, but the sex shop on the other side of the parking lot was open. He saw Paul and June Bryan, the couple who owned Essentia, through the front windows.

Fernando parked the Cherokee and set the brake. He walked to his office and opened the door, but he chose not to put the 'Open' sign in his window. Not today.

On his way to the desk he eyed his mini refrigerator along the wall. He kept it stocked with bottles of water for the mornings and Modelo for the afternoons. He checked his watch. Didn't happy hour come earlier on Sunday?

He fought the urge to grab a beer and instead sat down at his desk, noticing the light blinking on his phone. He had a message, one message. He hit the replay button and sat back to listen:

"Uh...Fernando, Fidel here. I wanted to let you know that Rodger Barkley has called an unexpected news conference on the steps of City Hall this afternoon at two o'clock. Rumor has it that he'll announce he's ending his campaign for a seat on City Council and his participation in the Take Back Our Streets movement. Looks like it's fallout from the Tryzinski scandal. Too much bad press. Anyway, I thought you might be interested in coming. I'll be covering it for the paper."

Well, well, Fernando thought. When the smoke clears from the Tryzinski scandal, who knows who'll still be standing.

Since the press conference was less than a half hour away, he postponed the Modelo and drove back downtown, this time parking in his usual spot on Alameda Street. He walked up the hill to San Francisco Street, along the side of the La Fonda Hotel, and then crisscrossed the Plaza to Lincoln Avenue. As he approached he saw a crowd gathered around the steps of City Hall, as before. This crowd looked and sounded more subdued than the last, even though he did see a few Take Back Our

Streets signs. Looked like no more than twenty or thirty supporters of Barkley who more than likely had heard rumors of Barkley's withdrawal from the City Council race. No protestors this time. Why protest a campaign that's ending?

On the street Fernando saw a KRQE TV news van with its antenna arm raised. The news crew, a cameraman and a broadcaster, stood next to Fidel in front of the steps to City Hall. A microphone had been set up there for Barkley to speak when he appeared. Fidel spotted Fernando and motioned for him to come join them, but Fernando stayed back where he could watch the entire crowd. He saw mostly sad, dejected faces in the crowd. Mostly men with hangdog expressions, not many women. None of them appeared all that angry, which was a blessing. Too much anger these days.

Minutes later Barkley stepped out of City Hall and walked to the microphone to muted applause from the crowd. Wearing a starched button-down white shirt and blue slacks, Barkley looked every inch like an experienced politician. In fact, Barkley was the portrait of a patrician: handsome, wealthy, well-educated, and seasoned from a lifetime of public service. An ambitious man caught in a rapidly developing scandal not of his making and out of his control.

Barkley brushed a lock of silver hair from his forehead and raised his hands. "Please...thank you all for coming. I'm sorry I don't have better news for you today. It's with a heavy heart that I'm announcing the end of my campaign for City Council. Events over the past few days have made it impossible for us to continue with our crusade to take back our streets. We simply cannot be heard over the outcry and the bad press resulting from one individual's illegal action. Illegal action that does not represent who we are as a movement."

The crowd responded with a collective groan.

Barkley raised his hands again. "No, our struggle is not over. I tell you here and now that our struggle will not be over until we succeed in taking back our streets. We will return, when the present tempest blows over. The truth of the matter is that the citizens of Santa Fe are with us even though many are afraid to say so under the present circumstances. We all want clean streets and parks, free from needles and garbage and human waste. We all want to stop the mob of criminals pouring into our city from south of the border. I make this promise to you: we will take back our streets, maybe not at this particular moment, but soon. Stay tuned."

Fidel's hand shot up in the air, waving at Barkley. "Mr. Barkley, hasn't the fact that Homer Tryzinski, the co-founder of your movement, housed and employed illegal immigrants exposed the hypocrisy of your campaign?"

Anger flashed across Barkley's face. "No comment."

With that, Barkley hurried back into City Hall while the crowd cheered half-heartedly. It was a stark ending to a campaign that at one time had promised to upend and reshape city politics.

The crowd disbursed slowly, Barkley's supporters ambling off to their cars and looking dejected. Fernando waited while Fidel and the KRQE reporter talked for a few minutes. Then the TV news crew packed up their camera equipment and carried it to their van. Fidel joined Fernando on the sidewalk.

"Good riddance, huh?" Fidel said.

Fernando nodded. "You want to get a beer downtown?"

"No can do," Fidel said. "I have to meet deadline. This will be the lead story in tomorrow's paper."

"Okay. Keep me informed," Fernando said.

Fidel jumped into his car and took off, while Fernando walked over to Alameda Street where he'd left his Cherokee. He decided not to go back to his office, so he made a U-turn on Alameda and took the Paseo up the hill to Acequia Madre.

He had a lot to tell Estelle. She would be happy to know that Barkley, like Tryzinski, had ended his anti-immigrant campaign for City Council. Maybe the air had finally gone out of the sails of the Take Back Our Streets movement. He hoped.

24

Monday morning Estelle blamed Fernando for her fuzzy head. They'd gone to La Choza last night to celebrate the demise of the Take Back Our Streets movement and Estelle, not a regular drinker, had enjoyed one too many glasses of white wine. She'd climbed out of bed in the middle of the night to pop an extra strength Tylenol and drink a large glass of water. By morning she still hadn't slept much. Still, she took her morning shower, dressed for work, ate her regular breakfast, and then passed out on the daybed in the living room wearing her work clothes, slacks and a long-sleeve paisley shirt.

Fernando tip-toed into the living room to check on her. He didn't dare wake her, not wanting to incur Estelle's wrath. Watching her sleep, he realized once again how lucky he was to have married a woman who had aged so beautifully. She looked twenty years younger than he did, slim and fit, with a delicately-featured face free of wrinkles. Her dark brown hair was streaked with touches of silver-gray, accenting her high forehead and the twist of her nose. Without that touch of silver-gray she would like one of his daughters!

When Fernando left the house at nine Estelle was still sleeping. He let her sleep and quietly closed the kitchen door behind him. He drove around the Paseo to Canyon Road and up to his office. The parking lot was empty this morning. Monday was usually a slow go on Canyon Road. It usually took a while for people to recover from their weekends. Come Noon people would start showing up on the street and in the galleries. By two or three o'clock even the bars and restaurants would be jumping.

He parked next to his Private Eye sign and walked down the gravel path to his office. Once he put his 'Open' sign in the window and sat down at his desk to read the morning *Independent*, he felt like he'd finally started his day. As Fidel had predicted, the lead story in the front section concerned Rodger Barkley's surprise announcement that he was ending his campaign for a City Council seat.

Halfway through Fidel's news story his cell phone rang. He

recognized the voice immediately:

"Lopez...can you hear me?" Wayne croaked. "Yeah, you better get up here fast. I saw that silver Toyota coming up Canyon Road again. Now there's shooting up at the old Forest Service building...sounds like all hell's breaking loose up there...hell if I know what's going on...you're the cop or whatever you call yourself these days, I don't know. Can you hear me?"

"I can hear you, Wayne," Fernando said and clicked off, not wanting to waste time.

He called Manny immediately. When Manny didn't answer, he left a message on Manny's phone asking for help.

Fernando took his Smith & Wessen out of the bottom drawer of his desk and grabbed an extra box of ammo. Then he locked up his office and climbed into his Cherokee. He raced out of the parking lot, spewing loose gravel as he turned onto Canyon Road and gunned the big engine.

Halfway to Upper Canon Road he began to have second thoughts. Why was he risking his life for people he didn't even know? Against the Sinaloa Cartel, no less? Then again, maybe he did have a horse in this race. He didn't want the cartel to get a footing in Santa Fe. Once the Sinaloa mafia took over a city, the city turned to shit. Somebody had to stand up to them. Manny and hopefully Antonio would be on their way. They had to be there, it was their job. He could at least help.

Fernando roared past Wayne's alley and then slowed down, trying to figure out how to play this. He could see the silver 4Runner far up on the hill. He couldn't just drive into the front yard of the A-frame with his Smith & Wessen blazing and expect the cartel gunmen to throw down their weapons. He needed an edge, or at least the advantage of surprise.

Off to his right he saw a cluster of piñon trees, maybe a hundred yards from the A-frame. That would have to do. He turned off the road and bounced across the rough mesa to the trees, which gave him enough cover to hide the Cherokee. As soon as he opened the door and stepped out of the driver's seat he heard a gunshot, followed by another. He ducked behind the Cherokee and waited, just to make sure the bullets weren't intended for him. Then, crouching, he eased up behind the trees. He had his Smith & Wessen in hand and his pockets full of ammo.

From behind the trees he saw what was happening up ahead. Two Sinaloa gunmen were hiding behind the 4Runner, which was parked on the left side of the parking area. They were firing at the A-frame about thirty or forty yards away. Someone, no doubt Ricardo, was firing back at them from a broken window. Sounded like all three of them were shooting with pistols, which meant their chances of hitting each other from that distance were minimal. That didn't last long. One of the gunmen, the big one, opened the rear of the 4Runner, took out what looked like an AR-15, and quickly inserted a clip.

Fernando watched events unfold, unsure of how to intervene. The big gunman raised his semi-automatic rife and steadied it on the roof of the 4Runner. Then he fired repeatedly:

THOK...THOK...THOK

The bullets shattered what was left of the window in the A-frame. Ricardo screamed inside and then went silent. Moments later Maria screamed. "Help me...help me!" she screamed.

Instantly the smaller gunman jumped out from behind the hood of the 4Runner. He waved his gun at his partner and shouted, "Cover me!"

The two gunmen walked toward the A-frame, the smaller one out front and the larger man lagging behind, providing cover with his AR-15. No defensive gunfire came from the A-frame now. Only Maria sobbing and then silence.

Suddenly Fernando heard a vehicle approaching on the rough road leading to the A-frame. He turned around and saw Manny's cruiser come racing down the road in a cloud of brown dust. Manny slammed on his brakes when he entered the parking area. The cruiser skidded to a stop on the right of the parking area, about the same distance to the A-frame as the 4Runner. Manny jumped out of the car with his weapon in hand, leaving the car door wide open.

"Drop your guns!" Manny shouted at the two gunmen. "Now!"

The large gunman spun around to face Manny, while the smaller continued walking toward the A-frame, ignoring Manny's order.

"I said throw down your guns!" Manny shouted again.

Instead, the big man dropped to one knee and fired two shots: THOK, THOK.

Manny managed to get off one wild shot before collapsing. He grabbed his midsection with both arms and fell to the ground.

Meanwhile, the smaller gunman walked into the A-frame. Maria started screaming again. There were sounds of a struggle inside the house.

When the big man turned to look at the A-frame, Fernando saw his opportunity. He burst out of the trees and ran toward the rear of Manny's cruiser, putting the cruiser between him and the gunman so as to disrupt the gunman's line of sight. He lunged the last few yards, smacking into the trunk of the cruiser. Then he laid low for a few moments, trying to get his breath.

Hearing the collision, the big man turned and raised his AR-15. He moved slowly, cautiously to his left, trying to spot whoever made the noise.

As the big man approached the left side of the cruiser, Fernando crouched low and moved to the right side. When Fernando came to the front of the cruiser he waited a couple of seconds and then popped up over the hood with his Smith & Wessen pointed at the gunman.

"Drop the fucking gun!" Fernando shouted as loud as he could.

The big man, surprised, jumped back and fired off a round that ricocheted off the roof of the cruiser.

Fernando fired one shot that hit the gunman in the lower chest. The big man stumbled and took a step toward Fernando before falling to his knees and trying to raise his AR-15.

Fernando fired again, the bullet striking the gunman in the upper chest. The big man fell face first into the dust.

Fernando moved quickly around the cruiser to the gunman and kicked him in the side. The gunman moaned faintly and then lay still, blood spreading out under both sides of his chest.

Just then Fernando heard Maria scream and saw her standing in the door of the A-frame. The smaller gunman stood behind her, holding a pistol to her head. The gunman pushed her outside and then wrapped his arm around Maria's neck. Like this the two of them stumbled and lurched their way across the parking area.

Fernando followed them with his Smith & Wessen. "Drop your gun, there's no way you can get away. More cops are on their way."

"Hah! We have safe houses all over Santa Fe County," the gunman said. "Stay out of my way or I'll put a bullet in her head."

Fernando lowered his gun and let them go, eyeing the gunman carefully. Maria and her captor shuffled over to the 4Runner and climbed inside. Moments later they roared down the hill, their dust swirling over the dirt road and forming a funnel cloud.

As soon as the 4Runner left, Fernando rushed to Manny's side. Manny's eyes were starting to glaze, but he managed a faint smile. "Fucker shot me in the gut," Manny said, holding his mid-section tightly to minimize blood loss.

Fernando didn't waste time. He dialed nine one one and then called Linda Stephens the dispatcher at the Washington Avenue Station. Within minutes he heard the sirens racing up Canyon Road.

The ambulance arrived first, followed closely by Antonio's cruiser. Two medics jumped out of the ambulance. They stabilized Manny, loaded him on a stretcher, and carried him to the ambulance. Seconds later Manny was en route to the Christus Saint Vincent Emergency Room. The rescue was completed so quickly that Fernando hardly had a chance speak to the medics.

Antonio parked behind Manny's cruiser. He struggled to get his six foot eight inch body out from behind the steering wheel. First thing he did was walk over to the body of the dead gunman. He bent over and picked up the AR-15. "Is this the guy who shot Manny?" Antonio asked.

"That's him," Fernando said.

"Is he dead?"

Fernando nodded.

"Good, then I don't have to kill him," Antonio said. "Did you get the license number of the 4Runner."

"No, but it was a Texas plate, with an El Paso dealer's license holder," Fernando said. "Silver, recent model."

"That should be enough," Antonio said. He called in and had the station issue an APB for the Toyota, noting that the driver was armed and dangerous and holding a woman, Maria Aragon, hostage.

Fernando pointed to the door of the A-frame. "Ricardo's inside. I think they killed him."

The two of them walked into the rustic cabin. Broken glass littered the floor of the front room. Ricardo's twisted body lay on the floor among the glass shards where he had fallen. One of the bullets had left a gaping hole in his left shoulder, revealing a shattered collar bone. Another bullet had pierced his forehead. Where the back of his skull should have been, there was only a pool of blood.

They stepped outside so Antonio could call Forensics. After alerting Forensics, Antonio turned to Fernando. "I'll need your statement."

Fernando nodded. "You want to meet me at the hospital?"

"I'll follow you," Antonio said.

25

Fernando and Antonio waited all afternoon at Christus Saint Vincent Hospital until Manny was out of surgery. The surgeons had to remove one kidney and a section of Manny's large intestine, both shredded by bullets from the AR-15. Antonio left as soon as Manny arrived in the ICU. The attending nurse assured them that Manny would recover and lead a normal life, whatever normal meant for a police detective. Fernando stayed in the waiting room down the hall from the ICU, waiting for a chance to visit Manny. Thirty minutes later the nurse reappeared with the news that he could visit Manny as long as he kept his visit brief.

Fernando hardly recognized the wise-ass, punkish Manny as he lay on his hospital bed, his face as pale as his hospital gown. Wires attached to Manny's body were hooked to machines that monitored his pulse, heart rate, and oxygen levels. Manny had IVs in both hands and drains on both sides of his abdomen. He looked gravely ill, even weaker than when Fernando last saw him back at the A-frame.

"Hey, buddy, how you doing?" Fernando asked, standing next to the bed.

Manny's eyes opened and tried to focus on Fernando. He seemed to come back from far away. He smiled faintly and then closed his eyes again.

"He's very weak," the nurse said. "He needs to sleep."

Fernando nodded. He gave Manny's hand a squeeze and then walked out of the ICU. It was too late to do much of anything now. Antonio had promised to call him as soon as the APB produced results. Surely someone in the Santa Fe area would see the silver 4Runner with Texas plates. It was just a matter of time, Fernando told himself. A waiting game.

On his way out of the hospital Fernando passed Manny's twin brother Juan and his wife Emily, who'd just arrived from Taos. Linda had called them earlier from the Washington Avenue Station. Juan and Emily were Manny's only family. Manny was a bachelor and lived alone in an apartment on Hyde Park Road.

"How is he?" Juan yelled from across the lobby.

Fernando had to take a second look. Manny and Juan were identical twins. It was like seeing Manny, risen from his ICU bed, walk through the double doors into the lobby. Fernando gave Juan a thumb's up.

Feeling out of sorts, all sixes and sevens, Fernando drove back to his office on Canyon Road and helped himself to a Modelo. Maybe a beer would help. Whenever something like this happened, he would brood for days on what had gone wrong, on what could have been done to prevent the tragedy. The brooding never helped. It was just that he had to blame himself in order to forgive himself. Or something convoluted like that.

After he finished his Modelo Fernando called it a day and drove home. Estelle was in the kitchen preparing dinner, a hot Green Chile Stew with an added tablespoon of powdered red chile from Chimayo, her go-to dish after a long, busy day. He told Estelle about Manny. After dinner they spent all of two hours on their patio talking about what happened. More brooding. But by the time they went to bed he was feeling a little better, or at least resigned. All the brooding in the world wouldn't change anything. Manny would still be lying in the hospital hooked to wall of machines.

Fernando knew he wouldn't be able to sleep, so he took one of Estelle's sleeping pills before bed. The sleeping pill helped, but he still tossed and turned at first, reliving the shoot-out at the A-frame. Over and over, until he finally fell asleep exhausted. When he awoke his mouth was dry and felt like it was stuffed with cotton. Groggy, he climbed out of bed and showered, hoping the hot water would jolt him awake. It helped, but two cups of coffee helped even more. Estelle had already left for work, so for breakfast he ate the leftover Green Chile Stew cold, too lazy to make himself a proper breakfast. By nine he was ready for the day.

Before leaving the house he called Antonio to check on developments.

"No, nothing much," Antonio said. "We got a call late yesterday afternoon from a woman who said she saw a gray or silver 4Runner while driving on Saint Francis Drive. Said she thought it was a 4Runner anyway. It crossed Saint Francis on West Alameda heading west."

"Hmmm...well, if there is a Sinaloa safe house in Santa Fe I would expect it to be west or south of the city," Fernando said.

"Exactly. So we're sending a patrol car down West Alameda every hour on the hour," Antonio said. "So far they've found nothing, but I'll let you know if anything changes."

With that, Fernando drove around the Paseo and up Canyon Road to his office. He killed time by reading the morning *Independent* and then went next door to shoot the breeze with Ruby. By Noon he was at odds and ends. Too much waiting around. So, desperate, he drove back around the Paseo to West Alameda Street and followed it past Saint Francis Drive into the burbs or the boonies, he didn't know what to call the sprawling mix of new developments and old farms. A mishmash of old and new. Give the wealthy newcomers time and there would be nothing left of the old Santa Fe that he knew as a child.

He drove slowly, carefully, looking this way and that for any sign of the 4Runner. Toward the end of West Alameda he came upon an old-fashion auto repair shop that gave him an idea. It was a cinderblock building oozing grease right out of the 1950s. An old Conoco gas pump from decades ago still stood out front, while in back an entire lot was jammed with junked cars and car parts, mostly engines up on blocks. The faded tin sign on front read 'Stu's Auto Repair.'

Fernando turned into the busted concrete entrance to Stu's. He saw an elderly man in denim overalls and CAT baseball cap working on an old International pickup from the 1970s, just before International stopped making the trucks. The mechanic had taken the rear tires off the truck and was replacing the brake pads. Squatting on the greasy concrete floor, the old timer turned to stare at Fernando as he climbed out of the Cherokee.

Fernando walked up to the single bay and said, "Afternoon. My daddy used to own a 1960 International back when I was a kid."

The mechanic smiled, a bone thin old man with no front teeth. His deeply wrinkled face was sunburned to the color of mahogany. "Damn fine truck."

Fernando nodded. "Yes, it was. He loved that old truck."

"What can I do for you?" the old timer asked.

"Just a question," Fernando said. "Do you know of any chop shops around here?"

The mechanic looked confused. "Chop shops? For that Cherokee?"

Fernando laughed. "Oh, no, not for my Cherokee. I have a friend who wants to recondition his new Mustang, if you know what I mean."

Now the mechanic studied Fernando, suspicious. He got to his feet slowly, painfully, grabbing his right knee. He seemed uncertain about how to respond. "No...not really...I haven't heard of any in these parts."

Fernando smiled, knowing the mechanic was lying. Didn't matter, because he'd gotten the information he wanted. "Okay, sorry to bother you."

The mechanic watched him walk to the Cherokee and drive off. When Fernando looked in the rearview mirror, the wiry old man was still standing in the bay watching him drive way.

Knowing a chop shop existed was one thing, finding it was another. Maybe Antonio had an informant who knew something about the market in stolen vehicles. It was worth a try.

Not willing to give up quite yet, Fernando turned around at Saint Francis Drive and drove the length of West Alameda a second time. Same results. No sign of the silver 4Runner. And other than 'Sal's Auto Repair,' he saw nothing that even vaguely resembled a chop shop.

Finally he gave up and drove back to his office. When he found no messages on his answering machine, he headed home. Enough was enough.

26

Fernando didn't hear from Antonio until the next day. He'd just come back to his office after having lunch with Ruby at El Farol when his cell phone rang. He sat at his desk and answered the phone.

"Fernando, we've had a couple of developments this morning," Antonio said. "A neighbor called in and said she heard gunshots on Camino Tranquillo, off West Alameda. Then the driver of a Waste Management garbage truck called saying he saw a dead body in front of a Quonset hut at the end of Camino Tranquillo."

"Never heard of the street," Fernando said.

"It's a small unpaved road off to your left as you come down West Alameda, not much there," Antonio said. "I'm on my way now. You want to meet me there? I don't trust anyone else for backup now that Manny's down. Be like old times."

Like old times. Fernando liked that. He and Antonio had a long history, most of it good. "I'll be there," he said and then locked the office, not bothering to change the sign to 'Closed.' He'd be back soon enough. He hoped.

He walked to the Cherokee and placed his Smith & Wessen in the glove compartment, just in case. Then he drove around to West Alameda Street and headed west. He missed Camino Tranquillo the first time he drove by, so he had to backtrack and slow down in order to find it on his second drive-by. Like Antonio said, there wasn't much on Camino Tranquillo. He saw a couple of older adobe houses at the entrance to the gravel road and a Quonset hut at the far end. The road itself ended at a large mound of gravel apparently used for maintaining the road.

Fernando turned into Camino Tranquillo and drove past the two houses, both of which had empty garbage bins in their driveways. The mid-afternoon sun reflected off the steel Quonset hut and blinded him momentarily. He raised his hand to block the glare, catching a glimpse of Antonio's cruiser parked on the side of the road. At first he didn't see Antonio. Then he saw the big man walking across the dirt parking lot in front of the Quonset hut toward what appeared to be a body lying in the dirt.

Fernando parked behind the cruiser and walked to join Antonio. They stood looking at the gruesome sight: a heavyset male with long black hair lying on his stomach. The corpse wore torn jeans and a tan shirt, both covered with bright splotches of paint, every color in the rainbow. In addition to paint, the tan shirt had been stained dark red by blood oozing out of three jagged, gaping holes in the corpse's back. The arms of the corpse reached out ahead of the body, its fingers dug into the dirt.

"Looks like someone shot him in the back while he was running away," Antonio said, "and then he tried to claw his way back to the Quonset hut."

Fernando nodded. "Did you call Forensics?"

"They're on their way," Antonio said.

While they talked dogs started barking from the nearest of the two adobe houses. They saw an elderly woman come out of the house and walk stiffly down the street toward them. Behind her a pack of dogs barked from her fenced-in back yard. She wore slacks and a simple cotton top, her long gray hair trailing behind her in the breeze as she walked. As she approached she waved at them.

"I been waiting for you, where you been?" the woman asked, her pale, thin face lined with wrinkles.

"We got here as soon as we could," Antonio said. "Can you tell us what happened here?"

The woman frowned. "They drove up and shot him. Two men in one of those big Rovers or whatever they're called."

"Range Rovers?" Fernando asked.

"Yeah, I guess," she said. "It was black. That's all I know."

"Do you recognize this man?" Antonio asked.

"Sure, that's Herb Meyer," the woman said. "He runs the garage there. Or did. He isn't gonna be running anything now, is he?"

"What kind of garage?" Antonio asked. "What kind of customers came here?"

"Nobody you'd wanna know," she said. "Mostly young men bringing in cars they wanted to sell real fast. He would 'fix' 'em, if you know what I mean. So they could be sold."

"Selling stolen cars, you mean," Fernando said.

The woman nodded. "I reckon. I kept my distance from that bunch. Don't know, don't care. That's what I think. Keep outta other people's business."

"Have you ever seen vehicles here with license plates from Mexico?" Antonio asked.

"Mexicans? Hell, no, that's all we'd need," the woman replied. She looked at the corpse and wrinkled her face. "So what are you gonna do with Herb? You can't just leave him lying in the dirt."

Antonio sighed. "We'll take him to the morgue and see if he has any kin who might want to claim the body."

She looked at Antonio and then at the body again. "Be easier just to throw him over my fence and let the dogs have him. He was no good."

Fernando fought to stifle a laugh. He and Antonio watched her turn and walk back to her adobe, the dogs greeting her with a crescendo of barking that was worse than listening to a pack of coyotes devouring a rabbit.

"That's rich," Antonio said, after she'd gone. "Throw him to the dogs."

"Easy clean up!" Fernando said in jest.

Antonio glanced at the Quonset hut. "Okay, let's check out the place. See what we can find."

Fernando followed Antonio into the steel building, divided into thirds. One third of the building consisted of a small office in front and a living space in back. The chop shop took up the other two thirds of the building. They found one bay and a network of winches and pulleys overhead hanging from steel rafters. On benches along the sides of the space were auto body repair tools, everything from saws, grinders, and sanders to stud welders and acetylene torches. Along the rear wall they found shelves of automotive paint and spray-painting equipment, including spray-painting guns and condensers. It was clear from the sheer amount of equipment that Herb Meyer had done a good, if illegal business.

When they heard a vehicle outside, Fernando followed Antonio out into the parking lot. The SFPD Forensic van pulled up behind Fernando's Cherokee and both Teresa and Miguel climbed out. Teresa headed for the corpse of Herb Meyer, while Miguel came over to talk.

"Fernando, damn, I think I see you as much now as I did when you were working for the department," Miguel said, a bird-like little man with a beak for a nose.

Fernando laughed. "Probably. Dead people just keep showing up in my line of work."

Teresa joined them, a heavy-set young woman with a winning smile. "It's true, you attract lotta dead people, Fernando."

"Hey, I'm just the middle man--they're dying to get to you!" Fernando said, joking.

Everyone laughed. Even Antonio cracked a smile, a rarity for the doggedly serious ex-Marine. Antonio quickly caught himself and said, "Okay, let's get to work then."

Fernando walked to the Cherokee, so as not to interfere with Miguel and Teresa's work. Antonio came after him.

"Who knows what the silver 4Runner looks like today, if it was in the chop shop last night," Fernando said.

Antonio frowned. "Looks like the work of the cartel, but we won't know for sure until we find out if Herb was shot by the same AR-15 that wounded Manny. It'll take twenty-four to forty-eight hours to get the ballistics report. I hate waiting."

"Copy that," Fernando said.

27

Antonio was right. There were still too many unknowns, starting with the whereabouts of Maria Aragon and ending with what happened to Herb Meyer on Camino Tranquillo. Fernando dreaded the unknown, because in his line of work what you didn't know usually came back to bite you in the ass. What bothered him most was the sudden arrival of the Sinaloa Cartel in Santa Fe. Maria's kidnapper had said back at the A-frame that Sinaloa already had several safe houses in Santa Fe County. If that was true, then the city of Santa Fe and its police department were woefully unprepared for the onslaught.

So far there had been no responses to he APB on the silver 4Runner. That told Fernando the kidnapper hadn't gone down I-25 to Albuquerque, where he likely would have been spotted by the highway patrol. Of course, the kidnapper could have taken Highway 14, the slow route to Albuquerque that curved around behind the Sandia Mountains. Or the kidnapper could have stayed put, hiding in one of the cartel's safe houses in Santa Fe and taking the silver 4Runner to a chop shop. Herb Meyer's chop shop.

Driving back to his office, Fernando resigned himself to the fact that all he could do now was wait for Maria to contact him, if she were still alive and could get free of her kidnapper. He had no control over events. He drove around the Paseo to Canyon Road and up to his office. As usual this time of day his parking lot was full of vehicles with Texas and Colorado license plates. Mobs of tourists roamed up and down Canyon Road in these last, dying days of summer.

Ruby waved at him from the front porch of her gallery, where she'd gone to smoke a cigarette. That surprised Fernando. Ruby had quit smoking about the same time he'd quit. At least now he knew where to go to bum a cigarette. What better time than now, he decided. So he walked over to Ruby's gallery and asked, "Can I bum one of those?"

Ruby took a long puff and then blew out white smoke. "I thought you quit?"

Fernando laughed. "I thought you did too."

"I did. Just like you. Here," she said, offering him a pack of Marlboros.

He took one cigarette and handed back the pack of cigarettes. "I'll save this for later. When I need it."

"Exactly what I do," Ruby said. "I just had a redneck from Oklahoma in here tell me that Jimmy's paintings were Satanic. I told him to get the hell out."

"That's a new one," Fernando said.

Ruby glanced at him. "I wish. You wouldn't believe some of the people who come in the gallery."

With that, Fernando walked down and unlocked his office door. He opened his windows to get rid of the stuffy, late afternoon smell that still plagued the ex-garage. He didn't dare leave them open when he was out. Leaving your windows open in this city was an invitation to trouble, trouble in the form of larcenists with guns, big guns.

Then Fernando took a can of Modelo out of his mini-refrigerator and sat at his desk, reflecting on his day. About half-way through the Modelo he saw dark shadows outside his door.

When the door burst open, a hipster with a gold chain dangling from his neck stepped inside. Fernando reached for his Smith & Wessen in the top drawer of his desk.

"Don't--you'll be dead before you can open the drawer," the man said curtly, nodding toward the two men behind him, tough looking goons wearing tight muscle shirts over their powerful bodies, their right hands behind their backs.

Fernando slowly brought his empty hand up to the desktop where it could be seen.

"Do you know who I am?" the hipster asked, a slick, handsome fellow with a new, days-old beard and perfectly coiffed hair who looked like someone you would meet at a craps table in the sleaziest casino in town. He wore a black shirt with the top two buttons open revealing his gold chain. His tight, pressed jeans barely fit over his cowboy boots made from some exotic animal probably killed and skinned just for his pleasure while he watched.

Fernando sighed. "I know who you are." He recognized Silva Archivada from the photos he'd seen on the nightly news: the alleged head of the Sinaloa Cartel in New Mexico.

"Good, then we have no illusions about who we are dealing with," the man said, smiling. "I know who you are, and you know who I am."

Fernando nodded, nervous.

"Now, it has come to my attention that you killed one of my men," Silva said, still smiling. "Not just any man, but one of my best. Eloy was my first lieutenant. So you see the gravity of my situation."

"Eloy killed Ricardo Aragon and wounded a police detective, who happens to be a friend of mine," Fernando replied, out of his comfort zone but damned if he would be intimidated by this sleaze-ball who looked like a common ordinary pimp. "So you see the gravity of my situation."

Silva nodded. "I do."

"So what do you want then?" Fernando asked, gaining confidence the longer their conversation continued.

"I'm here to make a deal, among equals," Silva said. "I am aware of your reputation, and I am sure you are aware of mine. Neither of us wants a war. So I come to you asking for a deal. For a truce."

"That's fine, but I can only speak for myself; I can't speak for the Santa Fe Police," Fernando said.

Silva nodded. "We are working on that."

I'm sure you are, Fernando wanted to say but didn't.

"The thing is, I am a legitimate businessman," Silva said. "I am not like poor Chapo, who was a thug and a reckless fool. I am legit. I own a nightclub in Las Cruces and one in Albuquerque. Now I will soon have one in Santa Fe, which is why I need peace. You see?"

Fernando frowned. "Peace? That's a big word."

"Yes, but it is possible, if we have an agreement," Silva said. "After all, we will soon be neighbors. I've just signed the papers to buy that Forest Service house the Aragons were renting. In addition to my nightclub."

"Where's your nightclub?" Fernando asked.

"We bought the old Line Camp out on Highway 285 in Pojoaque," Silva said. "It has many advantages, not the least that it is outside city limits, which gives us more, shall we say, freedom. We will mix your country music with our Tejano and Mariachi, maybe some Corrido."

Fernando raised his hand to stop Silva's sales pitch. "There is one thing. Maria Aragon. What did you do with her?"

"Ah yes, I expected you to ask about that woman," Silva said. He turned to his two goons. "Bennie, you want to give Mister Lopez our present?"

Bennie grunted something incomprehensible and walked to the desk. He dropped a small cloth doll on the desk and then walked back to the door.

Fernando picked up the doll, a New Orleans type voodoo doll with tiny symbols that looked Native American. A gold pin pierced the chest of the doll where the heart would be located. A skull's face was painted on the doll's face and attached to that was a lock of black hair.

"That is Maria's hair," Silva said sharply. He was no longer smiling. He no longer looked like a cheap thug.

"Where is she?" Fernando asked.

"She is with her own people, where she belongs," Silva said. "This is just a warning of what happens when we don't keep our truce."

With that, Silva turned and walked out the door. His two goons followed.

Fernando hurried to the door and watched them walk up the gravel path to a black Range Rover in the parking lot. He cursed out loud when he saw the black Range Rover. He should have guessed. Just like the neighbor woman at Herb Meyer's chop shop had told them.

He watched until they drove off on Canyon Road. Then he went back to his desk and picked up the doll, staring at the lock of Maria Aragon's hair.

28

After Silva and his gorillas left, Fernando finished his Modelo. He hated to get involved with Sinaloa, but after shooting Eloy he had no choice. He was involved whether he liked it or not. News that Silva had bought Line Camp and the old Forest Service building to use as bases of operations in Santa Fe only compounded the problem. Sinaloa would have a storefront, a physical presence in northern New Mexico. Silva called himself a legitimate businessman, but there was nothing legit about what Silva sold.

Fernando remembered Line Camp, a Wild West honky-tonk out in Pojoaque. The infamous saloon/dancehall had been closed for years, but at one time Line Camp was one of the area's hot spots. It attracted a combustible crowd of rednecks and cowboys, hippies and revolutionaries that often as not erupted in brawls or even gunfire in the parking lot. He especially remembered radical lawyer Raoul Garcia hanging out at Line Camp. In fact, back then Raoul would sometimes hold office hours there, bringing with him a dangerous clientele of down-and-out hippies, fire-bombing revolutionaries, and outright criminals. Over the years Raoul's class warfare had taken a different tact. These days he imploded the obscenely wealthy from the inside, by taking their money through exorbitant charges. Raoul was the best criminal lawyer in the state.

Fernando had fond memories of Line Camp. When he was single, before he married Estelle and settled down, he'd been something of a regular at Line Camp. Those were his badass years. Looking back to those years made him happy. He didn't regret one damn thing of his youthful hijinks.

Fernando waited for over an hour before leaving. He wanted to see for himself if Sinaloa had already set up shop at his old honky-tonk. He locked up the office and drove down to the Paseo and around to Highway 84/285 West. The highway took him out of town past the Santa Fe Opera and the turnoff to the village of Tesuque. A few miles later he came to Buffalo Thunder, the huge casino resort owned by the Pojoaque Pueblo. Just beyond Buffalo Thunder the highway split, Highway 502 heading west toward Los Alamos, and Highway 84/285 shooting north toward Española and Taos. Line Camp was on the left side of 84/285 as it rounded the turn heading north.

Fernando looked for a parking lot or a fast food joint where he could pull over and observe Line Camp with his binoculars. He found a gas station situated at the bottom of a small rise, so he pulled into the station and drove behind the building. No one was around to bother him, so he took his binoculars out of the glove compartment and walked up the hill, through a patch of tumbleweed and snake grass that clung to his pants and socks and itched like hell.

The rise was just high enough for him to see over the commercial claptrap along the highway. He had a clear view of Line Camp, its front windows partly boarded up. The building seemed to sag in the middle as though tired, worn out from too many years and too much dancing. He saw two vehicles parked out front. One was a Griegos Construction panel truck with a ladder on its roof, indicating that renovations had already started. The other was a red SUV with a luggage rack on its top. Using his binoculars he saw the SUV had a temporary license from a dealer, with the paper document taped to the rear window. Suddenly it occurred to Fernando that he was looking at the silver 4Runner, painted red at Herb Meyers chop shop with a luggage rack on top and a fake temporary license added to conceal the identity of the Toyota. Not a bad job, not a bad job at all. He had to hand it to these guys, however begrudgingly.

Fernando stood on the hill watching for anyone leaving the building. Several minutes later the front door opened and two people walked out. The first person carried a metal clipboard in his hand, which told Fernando he was from Griegos Construction gathering information for an estimate. The second person looked familiar, too familiar for comfort.

Fernando focused the binoculars on the man's face and recognized the short man with the rat-like face who had kidnapped Maria Aragon back at the A-frame. Long time no see.

While Fernando watched, the Griegos Construction guy climbed into his panel truck and drove off down the highway toward Santa Fe. Likewise, Rat-face locked the front door of the building and drove off in the red Toyota.

Fernando made a split decision to follow the red Toyota. He half ran, half slid down the hill to his Cherokee and tossed his binoculars on the passenger seat. He fired the Cherokee's big engine and then drove around the gas station to the highway entrance. He waited until the red Toyota came around the long curve and then eased out onto the highway. He stayed back, not wanting to get too close. The red Toyota never went over the speed limit, which meant that Fernando had to drive much slower than he usually did. It took them an inordinate amount of time to reach Santa Fe.

In Santa Fe Rat-face turned off the highway onto Agua Fria Street, which here ran alongside the Santa Fe River. Fernando followed at a snail's pace. The red Toyota drove through the village of Agua Fria and entered a desolate stretch with open mesa on both sides of the road. Finally, after creeping along for miles, the red Toyota turned right into driveway beside a sprawling old farmhouse that looked out on an idle field on the other side of the road. The farmhouse had seen better days. The adobe and cement block structure had a rickety porch in front and a sloped tin roof with a weathervane on top.

Fernando drove past the farmhouse, careful not to glance at it or the red Toyota. About a mile down the road he turned around in a driveway and headed back. He passed the farmhouse again and then looked for a place to park along the river. He found a graveled pull-over about one hundred yards beyond the farmhouse. The pull-over offered a picnic table and a nearby garbage bin, neither of which he needed. What he did need was the cover provided by trees along the riverbank.

Easing into the pull-over Fernando parked the Cherokee out of sight of the farmhouse. Then he opened the rear compartment of the Cherokee, where his fishing equipment had been stored since his last fishing trip in the Pecos with Antonio. The fishing equipment would provide a needed disguise in case he was noticed. So he put on his fishing vest and assembled his rod and reel. A UNM cap pulled down low on his forehead completed the outfit. Even though the Santa Fe River was more a rivulet than a river, there were always a few optimistic fools who tried fishing there. Today he would be the fool.

Fernando ambled down to the river carrying his rod and reel. He scoured the river bottom as he moved slowly downriver, looking for fishing holes. He pretended to check out certain spots where there were actual pools of water. He stopped at one bend in the river to attach a fly and drop a line, all the while sneaking glances at the farmhouse. As he came closer he saw two men sitting on a patio behind the house overlooking the river. The two men seemed to be having an animated conversation about something. One of them was Rat-face. The other one he'd never seen, a big man wearing a camouflage shirt and jeans.

While Fernando pretended to fish, he heard a woman shout from inside the house. Even though muffled by a gag, the voice sounded like Maria's. He saw Rat-face jump up and rush inside, then the sharp sound of a slap, followed by silence. When Rat-face came back to the patio he was cursing. The big one said something that made Rat-face laugh. A real comedian.

Fernando had heard and seen enough. He turned around and shuffled back down the river toward the Cherokee, still pretending to look for fishing holes.

Apparently Maria Aragon was still alive. The problem now was how to get her out of that house, away from the Sinaloa bunch. He needed a plan, if not a SWAT team. He had neither.

29

On the way home Fernando stopped at Christus Saint Vincent to see Manny. In the past he'd only had occasion to visit the hospital's morgue or emergency room, so he went first to the front desk to get directions. Then he took the elevator to the designated floor and found Manny's private room across from the nursing station. Antonio was already sitting in a chair next to the bed, his long legs extended, taking up half the floor space in the room. Antonio smiled when he saw Fernando in the door, as if relieved that he would no longer be the only one there to make small talk with Manny. Antonio was not a great conversationalist.

Manny had his bed elevated so that he was sitting up. He still had one IV with the drip stand next to the bed, but he'd been disconnected from the beeping machines that had monitored his vital signs after surgery. Pale and weak, Manny looked like he'd been through the wringer. His eyes kept closing as if he were too tired to keep them open. Or maybe just bored with Antonio's presence.

"So this is where you're hiding," Fernando said. "Anything to avoid work."

Manny opened his eyes and smiled at Fernando. "They stole one of my kidneys. I saw them right before they put me out. Women docs hovering over me like a bunch of witches."

Fernando laughed. "I see you're not as exhausted as you look."

"I'm bored shitless," Manny said. "Look at me. Even if I could get out of bed, how could I escape wearing this damn hospital gown?"

"No way," Fernando said. "What's your hurry? Take it easy. Make sure everything's healing like it's supposed to. Antonio here can pick up the slack."

"That's true," Antonio said. "The Chief's already yelling at me. He's all discombobulated over this Sinaloa situation. Worried that we don't have the firepower to deal with a cartel. I think he's trying to look the other way, to pretend it isn't happening. The only detective we have left is Armando, the new guy from Colorado. He doesn't know shit about Santa Fe. Plus he's worthless."

Manny rolled his eyes.

"Give the guy some time to adjust," Fernando said. "Santa Fe's a tricky place, with three cultures and over four hundred years of history, some of it not very pleasant. It takes a while to find your way."

Antonio shrugged. "Let's hope he does."

"So Manny, what are they telling you about when you can leave?" Fernando asked.

Manny moved his head from side to side. "Maybe the day after tomorrow. If all goes well. Looks like I'll have to take extended sick leave. A couple of months anyway."

Fernando nodded.

"I don't know, maybe I'll just quit," Manny continued. "This episode has put the fear of God in me finally. I don't know if I want to risk another shooting, now that I'm down to one kidney. Especially with the Sinaloa coming to Santa Fe. We're so short-staffed."

"That's the thing," Antonio added. "The Mayor and the Chief just don't get it. We're way understaffed at the moment. They can't--or won't--find the money to bring in more officers."

"By the way, what happened to the sonofabitch who shot me?" Manny asked.

Fernando smiled. "You don't have to worry about him any more."

"Dead?" Manny asked.

"Dead," Fernando said. "That's the good news. The bad news is that several more thugs from Sinaloa are in town."

Fernando told them about Silva Archivada's visit, that Silva and two of his men had shown up in his office claiming he'd bought the old Line Camp, where he intended to run a legit business. Finally he told them about finding Maria Aragon at the Sinaloa safe house on Agua Fria Street.

Antonio looked surprised. "She's alive?"

"I think so," Fernando said. "I heard a woman shouting inside the house. It sounded like Maria. Looks like she's being held there by two men. One of them is the guy who kidnapped her back at the A-frame."

While they talked a smiling young nurse came into the room and said, "Hello, Mister Alvarez, are you behaving yourself?"

Manny beamed. He introduced the young woman as Erin. "I can't misbehave without you, Erin."

Erin laughed, a shapely brunette with shoulder length hair. She walked over to his bedside and checked his IV and then flushed the line with a syringe of saline solution. All business.

"So Erin, I think you may be the woman of my dreams," Manny said, wide awake now. "How's about we go out as soon as I get outta this place?"

Erin laughed. "You know it's against hospital policy for me to date a patient." She looked Manny over and winked. "Tell you what, when you're discharged I'll give you my phone number."

"Thanks," Manny said. "You're a life saver. I feel better already. I think I'm ready to leave."

"Uh-huh...you just take it easy so you can heal," she said, and ducked out of the door.

Manny turned to Fernando and Antonio. "You think she's serious."

"Probably not," Antonio said.

"I think so," Fernando countered. "Didn't you see her wink?"

Soon Erin returned with Manny's dinner tray, bringing an end to their visit. Fernando and Antonio left Manny with Erin and took the elevator down to the ground floor. They stopped for a few minutes in the parking lot to talk. They made tentative plans for how to get Maria out of the safe house on Agua Fria and then went their separate ways on the long day's journey into night.

30

Their plan was simple. Antonio would drive to the safe house and knock on the front door. Somehow Antonio would create a disturbance on the porch that would attract both of the Sinaloa thugs. Meanwhile, Fernando would park at the pull-off along the river and walk to the back patio. When Antonio created the distraction, Fernando would enter the house and rescue Maria. Then Fernando and Maria would run back to the Cherokee and drive away. As simple as that.

Antonio had to be in court at ten o'clock, so they set their meeting for Noon. They decided to meet at Alto Park, just off Agua Fria Street. Fernando was the first to arrive. He waited for Antonio at the entrance to the park. Ten minutes later, still waiting, he got bored and climbed out of his Cherokee to stretch his legs. He walked a ways into the park and then returned when he saw Antonio's cruiser pull up behind the Cherokee. Antonio rolled down his window and said, "Fucking judges. Another shooter got off with time served and a fine."

Fernando shook his head. "It's getting harder and harder to lock up criminals, so why even bother to arrest them?"

Antonio ignored Fernando's question and asked, "How do you want to do this?"

"Follow me down Agua Fria," Fernando said. "About a mile down there's a pull-off on the right along the river. Stop there and let me walk up behind the house before you proceed."

Antonio saluted.

Fernando jumped into the Cherokee and drove down Alto Street and turned left on Camino Alire, which took him directly to Agua Fria. He signaled a right turn as he approached the pull-off. Antonio parked behind the Cherokee and waved.

Fernando walked along the river toward the safe house. At this distance he couldn't see anyone on the back patio. The river glistened in the mid-day sun, not a cloud in the sky. With no breeze and no traffic on the street, the day was perfectly still. He could hear himself breathing. In and out.

That changed when he came closer. Surprised, he saw a white VW camper van parked in front of the house instead of the red Toyota. It looked like Maria and Ricardo Aragon's camper, the one he saw at the old Forest Service building on Upper Canyon Road. Same color.

When he came to the back patio and saw the Mexican license plate on the VW camper, he knew for sure. But why? What was the Aragon's VW camper doing here at a Sinaloa safe house?

Fernando stopped at the corner of the house and waved at Antonio, still parked on the pull-off. Moments later Antonio's cruiser came barreling down Agua Fria and skidded into the drive alongside the VW camper.

While Antonio went to the front porch, Fernando headed for the back door.

Antonio began pounding on the front door. When no one answered he pounded harder and then shouted, "Open the door or I'll kick it open!" Still no one answered.

Fernando didn't know what to do. He was supposed to wait until the front door opened and Antonio confronted the occupants. He tried the back door anyway but found it locked tight. He took out his lock pick and opened the door, but quickly saw that no one was inside.

Antonio had stopped banging and shouting now, so Fernando locked the back door and walked around front to join him. On his way Fernando checked out the VW camper, with the familiar Chihuahua license plate from Mexico. Looking through the side windows he saw plastic bags filled with painting supplies and a canvas clothes hamper overflowing with clothes.

"What do you think?" Antonio asked, standing on the porch.

Fernando glanced at the street. "Let's take a look inside the house." He took out his lock pick again and went to work on the front door. When the lock clicked open, Fernando stepped inside the house. Antonio followed. They paused a moment to let their eyes adjust to the room, darkened by closed windows and heavy curtains. Clearly the occupants wanted their secrecy.

The front room resembled a flophouse, with two sagging sofas facing one another and a scattering of cardboard boxes set up as side tables between them. Sleeping bags and dirty clothes hung on the backs of the sofas. Ashtrays, pipes, and empty beer cans littered the cardboard boxes. The floor was filthy with mouse droppings and dead insects. The room smelled vaguely of smoke and perspiration.

"Anyone here?" Fernando asked, just to be sure.

There was no response.

Fernando and Antonio moved into the kitchen, which overlooked the back patio. A metal folding table and two folding chairs stood in the center of the room. A Coleman camp stove and light-weight aluminum pans covered the kitchen counter, with a stack of paper plates and Styrofoam cups on a shelf above the counter. A Coleman cooler sat on the floor.

From the kitchen they moved into the one bedroom, which also reeked of sweat and something else. Disinfectant? An ancient brass bed wobbled in the center of the room as Fernando walked across the creaky wooden floor. He ignored a sheet and blanket twisted together on the bed, as well as a dirty gray pillow with a torn pillowcase. Something else caught his attention: a pair of handcuffs fastened to the brass railing of the headboard.

"Looks like they had Maria cuffed to the bed," Fernando said, rattling the handcuffs.

On the floor beside the bed lay a suitcase full of women's clothing.

"Yeah, and take a look at this," Antonio said, pointing to several paintings stacked upright and leaning against the rear wall of the bedroom. Oil paintings, all of them on strung canvases. None of them were yet framed.

Fernando came over to take a closer look. He picked up the first and saw Ricardo Aragon's signature in the lower left corner. He rifled through the rest and saw Ricardo's signature on all of them. He counted a total of five 24 x 36 canvases.

Antonio looked puzzled. "What do you make of that?"

"They must be selling them," Fernando said.

"Even like that? Not framed?" Antonio asked.

Fernando shook his head. "Sure, because Blaine can frame them. His gallery is the only place in town that sells Ricardo's paintings."

"Picasso and Co.?"

Fernando nodded. "I guess we better pay Blaine a visit and find out what's going on."

Antonio turned to go.

"Be sure to put everything back the way you found it," Fernando said. "If they find out we've discovered their safe house, they won't be back."

They walked through the rooms again, just to make sure nothing was disturbed. On the way out they locked the door from the inside and then closed it behind them.

"You want to meet at Picasso and Co.?" Fernando asked.

Antonio shook his head. "I really can't. We have a meeting with the Chief at two o'clock and I need to do some paperwork before the meeting. He's already on my ass for missing deadlines."

"Okay, let's keep in touch. Anything breaks with Sinaloa, let me know right away."

Fernando watched Antonio back up his cruiser and then take off fast, shooting out into Agua Fria and heading downtown. Then he walked slowly back to his Cherokee, parked in the pull-off. He kept thinking that Blaine might hold the key to what had become of Maria. Problem was, Blaine could be difficult. Like Ruby, his landlord, Blaine wasn't all that fond of the police or private investigators. Blaine could withhold information or fabricate when it was in his best interest to fabricate. Fernando had never really trusted Blaine, especially after the Jimmy Mackey case.

Even so, Fernando had no other lead at the moment, so when he reached his Cherokee he drove directly around to Canyon Road and parked in the side lot next to Picasso and Co.

Fernando noticed the banner over the gallery door, similar to the one Blaine hung after Jimmy Mackey had died: "The Last Paintings of the Late Great Ricardo Aragon." Good old Blaine, always trying to make a quick buck when one of his artists kicked the bucket. Opening the gallery door Fernando noticed the wall where Ricardo's paintings had been grouped was nearly empty.

Inside, Fernando heard Blaine talking to customers in the back office. Blaine escorted the customers, an elderly couple, out of the office into the gallery. The elderly man carried a large painting wrapped in sheets of brown paper.

"Are you sure you don't need help with that?" Blaine asked, as loud and boisterous as ever.

Dressed as quirky as usual, Blaine wore his red Bermuda shorts and a white T-shirt with a turquoise necklace around his neck. He looked and acted as wild and maniacal as England's Prime Minister, Boris Johnson, except more ominous. His dark hair stuck out in every direction, making him appear unhinged. Which matched his voice, always a few decibels louder than it needed to be.

"No, I'll be fine," the man said, eager to get away from mad Blaine.

Blaine escorted the couple out and held the gallery door open. Then he spun around to face Fernando and clapped his hands. "Damn! Everyone loves Ricardo's work. They sell faster than I can put them on the wall, at ten thousand dollars a painting."

Fernando didn't understand. "Why are they so popular?"

"Fuck if I know, old boy," Blaine said. "Must be the bright splotches of color. Like they're buying a Kandinski or something. Who knows? Art is subjective. Some people buy a painting just because its color matches their sofa. You gotta love art. Give a monkey a paintbrush and some asshole will buy it!"

"Nice to see you think so highly of your clientele," Fernando said sarcastically.

"Hah! As long as they buy the stuff, I love 'em! I just need to get more of Ricardo's work so I can keep the good times rolling."

Fernando nodded. "Maria has more of his paintings."

"Yeah, I know," Blaine said. "She stopped by this morning with two more canvases I still have to frame. As Ricardo's wife, she wants the proceeds––minus my twenty percent, of course. She came with this other guy, a squint-eyed little fucker who seemed more interested in the money than she did. Pushy little prick. He wanted me to charge twice as much for the paintings. I told him hell no, Ricardo might have something of a reputation in Mexico, but not here. When he kept on I 'bout grabbed the fucker by the neck and shook him. He shut his trap finally when he saw I meant business."

Fernando laughed. Blaine could be intimidating. Not only was he a loose canon, he stood six feet four inches and weighed two hundred and fifty pounds. The only person who wasn't intimidated by Blaine was Antonio, who had him by four inches and thirty pounds.

"Still, watch out for this guy," Fernando said. "He works for the Sinaloa Cartel. He's the guy who kidnapped Maria at the Forest Service building after Ricardo was murdered."

"No shit. That little runt?" Blaine said. "Are they all that small?"

"Hah! The two Sinaloa guys who came to my office with Silva Archivada were just as big as you, maybe bigger," Fernando said. He told Blaine about Silva's visit and that Silva had bought the Forest Service building on Upper Canyon Road.

That caught Blaine's attention.

"Not only that, Archivada bought the old Line Camp out in Pojoaque," Fernando continued. "He says he's turning it into a nightclub and intends to run a legitimate business."

"Great! Next he'll probably buy that other property on Canyon Road that's for sale," Blaine said. "I could see it now. Sinaloa could go toe to toe with Sotheby's for ownership of Santa Fe. Sotheby's might have more money, but Sinaloa has more guns. Money versus guns, who do you think would win?"

Fernando shook his head. "I think I better get out of here. Just be careful."

With that, Fernando walked out of Picasso and Co.

As he left he heard Blaine say behind him: "Fuck! I need to get out my Glock."

31

Fernando waited in his office until after five o'clock before driving around to again check the safe house on Agua Fria. When he saw the red Toyota wasn't parked in front of the house, only the Aragon's white VW camper van, he turned into the pull-off along the river. Frustrated, he berated himself. Why was he so concerned about the welfare of Maria Aragon? She wasn't a friend, she wasn't even a paying customer, so why did he care? She meant nothing to him. Not only that, but now that she was selling Ricardo's paintings for big bucks she'd have enough money to pay the cartel what they demanded and, hopefully, get out of town safely. End of story.

Enough, he decided. Let Maria take care of her own affairs. He had no interest in taking on the Sinaloa Cartel. Let the Santa Fe Police and the Feds handle the cartel. That was their job.

So, resigned, Fernando drove back around the Paseo to Acequia Madre and pulled into his driveway. Estelle's Camry was already parked in their one-car garage, which surprised him. She'd been working long hours for the Saint Francis Immigrant Outreach Program and coming home much later. He parked in the driveway and closed the garage door before walking into the house. He knew something was up when he found Estelle standing at the kitchen counter cooking a big meal and drinking a glass of her favorite wine, an Oregon pinot noir.

"What's the occasion?" Fernando asked.

"I'm celebrating," Estelle said. "We found out today that we got the corporate donation we applied for last Spring. They're giving us half a million dollars and the state is kicking in another hundred thousand. We'll finally have enough funds to help our people with rent, as well as food and clothing and medical care. I feel like we've turned the corner. We finally have enough funding, and we don't have to worry about the Take Back Our Streets people because both of their city council candidates withdrew from the race. That whole nightmare is over, at least for the moment. So, yeah, that's why I'm celebrating."

"Congratulations. That's great news," Fernando said.

"Oh, and the city is giving us a booth at the upcoming Fiesta," Estelle added. "We'll be able to recruit and solicit donations at Fiesta."

Fernando nodded. "Good exposure. I can't remember how many people attend Fiesta, but it's in the hundreds of thousands."

Estelle finished her glass of wine and set it in the sink. "What about you? What are you working on these days? You haven't mentioned anything since Wayne Fontenot saw the Devil on Canyon Road," she said, laughing.

"Not much," Fernando said. He'd told her about Manny being wounded, but not the details, and he wasn't about to tell her that Silva Archivada and the Sinaloa Cartel had arrived in Santa Fe. He didn't want to spoil her celebration, so he said nothing. "What are you making?"

Estelle smiled. "My Cuban pork roast, the one you like. I marinate the pork in orange and lime juices and then cook it with lots of garlic, oregano, and red chile pepper. Served with black beans and paella."

"Love it," Fernando said. He washed his hands and helped Estelle prepare the food.

"Here," Estelle said, pouring him a glass of wine. "I can't drink any more wine, not after my hangover the other day, but you should enjoy a glass."

After dinner Estelle went outside on the patio while Fernando put away the food and washed the dishes. He drank a Modelo as a nightcap while he did the dishes. Then he joined Estelle on the patio, where they enjoyed some quiet time together and watched the fireflies under the cottonwood trees along the acequia. He already felt a chill in the air on these late Summer evenings. Most people didn't realize that Santa Fe, with an elevation of 7,000 feet, could get damn cold during the Fall and Winter months.

Later they went to bed, Estelle first as usual. It took Fernando longer because he had his nighttime ritual of going through the garage first and then the house making sure the doors and windows were all closed and locked, except the windows in their bedroom, which they liked to keep open for the night breeze. Call him paranoid, but lately there had been a rash of burglaries on Santa Fe's trendy East side. He did what he could to secure his property.

Estelle was already snoring when he crept into the bedroom, tossed off his clothes, and crawled into the bed beside her.

Fernando slept like a baby, the best sleep he'd had in days. He felt free of worries about Maria. Unburdened. He dreamed of camping at Canjilon Lakes with his two daughters when they were young, one of his favorite memories. Fishing and hiking during the day, cooking over the campfire at night. Happy times. When he awoke, he was disappointed that it was all a dream. Sometimes he longed for those times when the girls were still at home and he and Estelle were young and in love.

The sight of Estelle still sleeping confused him. He checked the clock on the bedside table. Nine o'clock. Estelle never slept past six, and yet there she lay sound asleep. He moved away slowly, trying not to disturb Estelle.

Once out of bed he grabbed his clothes from yesterday and carried them to the living room, where he dressed and then splashed water on his face in the hallway bathroom. He frowned at his reflection in the mirror. Every time he looked at himself he questioned whether that image was really of him. He didn't feel as old as he looked, with his sunburned, wrinkled face and graying hair. He still thought of himself as middle aged, but his reflection said otherwise. Time was a mystery.

Now that he was dressed, he went to the kitchen and made coffee. His head was a little fuzzy this morning, but the coffee helped. He made himself an egg and toast and then had a second cup of coffee. By the time he heard Estelle stirring in the bedroom the clock on the kitchen wall showed ten o'clock. She came shuffling down the hallway into the kitchen wearing a silk robe and slippers. Her short gray hair was spiked up in all directions.

"I decided to sleep late this morning," Estelle said. "Time to slow down. I've been working too hard lately. Maybe I'll follow your lead. Take it easy for a change."

Fernando smiled. "Good. You deserve it, especially after these grants."

Estelle poured herself a cup of coffee and headed back down the hallway to the bedroom. Seconds later he heard the shower running.

Fernando turned to take his coffee out to the patio when his cell phone rang, ending his peaceful morning. With some trepidation, he answered the phone.

"Mister Lopez!" came Maria's hysterical voice. "Can you help us? Please! Mister Blaine just shot Diego in the head. We're at the gallery here. We don't know what to do!"

"What? Blaine shot him?" Fernando asked.

"Diego's dead!" Maria wailed.

"Where are you? At Blaine's gallery?" Fernando asked.

"*Si*," Maria sobbed.

"I'm on my way," Fernando said.

32

Fernando scribbled a note for Estelle and left it on the kitchen counter. He walked quietly to the laundry room and grabbed a sponge mop, a bottle of Clorox, a pack of latex gloves, a fistful of plastic bags, and two rolls of paper towels. Then he carried everything out to the Cherokee and placed the supplies in the rear compartment. He placed his Smith & Wessen in the glove compartment and checked to see if it was loaded. It was, so he climbed into the Cherokee. Still in a daze, with his head spinning, he raced down to the Paseo and around to Canyon Road. Minutes later he pulled into the parking lot alongside Picasso and Co. Thankfully, the parking lot was empty except for the red Toyota.

Fernando pulled in behind the red Toyota. He jumped out of the Cherokee and ran to the door of the gallery. The door was locked, so he pounded hard on the heavy door until he heard a dry click. Then the door swung open and Blaine stood before him, looking unhinged. Sweating profusely, his T-shirt smeared with blood, he glared angrily at Fernando.

"Hold the door open," Fernando said, ignoring the hostile look on Blaine's face. He ran back to the Cherokee, opened the rear compartment, and grabbed his supplies, which he then carried into the gallery.

"Now lock the door and keep it locked," Fernando said. "Don't let anyone in until we're finished here. Don't even answer the door."

Inside, Fernando saw Maria sitting in the office with a look of horror frozen on her face. She didn't speak or move when she saw Fernando approach.

Stepping into the office Fernando saw Diego lying on his back, with his arms flayed out and an automatic pistol near his right leg. Looked like a Glock. Everybody had a fucking Glock these days.

Fernando saw the cause of death immediately: a black hole in the center of Diego's forehead. A huge pool of sticky red blood had formed under what remained of the back of Diego's blasted skull.

"Jesus Christ, Blaine, what happened?" Fernando asked.

Blaine sighed. "The little fucker threatened me, demanded I give him one hundred percent of the sales. He even wanted me to pay him for the ones he just brought in today," Blaine said, pointing to the wall where the Ricardo paintings Fernando had seen at the safe house on Agua Fria Street were stacked, leaning against the wall. Still unframed.

"I told him he was fucking crazy, I wasn't going to pay him for paintings I hadn't even sold," Blaine added. "Plus I get twenty percent of the sales and if he didn't like it he could take a fucking hike. I'm not going to be intimidated by these little Mexican pricks."

"What happened next," Fernando asked.

"He pulled a gun on me, that's what happened," Blaine said. "Then Maria gasped and he turned to look at her. When he did, I pulled my gun out of the cubby hole on my desk and shot the fucker in the forehead, right between the eyes."

"Where did you learn to shoot like that?" Fernando asked, impressed by Blaine's ability to handle a gun. This was a side of Blaine he knew nothing about.

"In the Army, where do you think," Blaine responded. "I was in the Army for about six months when I was in my twenties, before they threw my ass out. Seems I had a bad attitude."

Fernando stared at Blaine.

"Dishonorable discharge," Blaine added. "I got tired of this one sergeant riding me all the time, so I decked him. When he got up, I decked him again. This time he didn't get up. I'll tell you the whole story some time."

"Where's your gun now?" Fernando asked.

Blaine reached in his desk and pulled out the pistol.

Fernando shook his head. "Another Glock, of course. Is this registered to you?"

"No, it's not registered," Blaine said. "I bought it at a gun show in Albuquerque from some sleazeball in the parking lot. Probably stolen."

"Good. Now listen to me," Fernando said. "I want you to hike up one of the trails into the national forest this afternoon and bury the gun somewhere no one will ever find it. Or, if you'd rather, drive down to Cochiti Lake tonight and toss the gun in the lake after dark, when you're sure no one's around to see you."

Blaine frowned. "Just what I want to do--go for a fucking hike."

Fernando shrugged. "Or you could take your chances. After we get done here, you'll probably be okay."

Maria broke her silence, sounding shell-shocked. "Do you want I call the Police?"

"No, no police," Fernando said. "Just follow my instructions, okay? First, I want one of you to bring me the eight by ten rug that's in the gallery. Right now. We need to act fast."

Mumbling to himself, Blaine went to the gallery and brought the rug into the office. He spread it out next to Diego's body.

Fernando put on a pair of latex gloves and rummaged through Diego's pockets until he found the keys to the red Toyota. He deposited the keys in one of the plastic bags he'd brought with him and put the bag in his pocket. Only then did he roll the body over onto the rug. He placed Diego's pistol next to him and then rolled up the rug with the corpse and the pistol inside. Then he pulled the rug and its contents into the gallery to get it out of the way.

Fernando stood up straight and stretched his back, which had begun to bark. "Okay, now I need two large paper bags and a bucket of warm water and soap. The bags need to be paper."

"I'll get them," Blaine said and disappeared through the rear door. He went next door to the casita where he lived and brought back two large paper bags from Albertsons and a bucket of warm, foamy water.

Fernando went to work. He placed layers of paper towels over the pool of blood on the floor. Layer after layer until only a red smudge remained on the tile floor. He stuffed the blood-soaked paper towels in the Albertsons bags, being careful not to get blood on his arms or his clothing. Then he pushed the two paper bags toward Blaine and said, "Okay, put these in the kiva fireplace over in the corner and burn them one at a time. Make sure everything burns. Then scrape the ashes out and flush them down the toilet."

Blaine reached for the bags.

"Not so fast," Fernando said, and tossed Blaine a pair of latex gloves. "Put these on, and when you're done cleaning out the ashes, wash the fire pit with soap and then burn a few newspapers to make it look used."

Blaine shook his head. "Fuck me! What are you now, a fixer?"

Fernando sighed. "I guess so."

While Blaine took care of the bags, Fernando washed the affected part of the floor with his mop, first with soapy water and then with Clorox. He waited a few minutes and washed the floor again with soapy water.

Then he carefully wiped the floor dry with more paper towels. Finally he removed the sponge from the mop and took the dirty sponge and the wadded up paper towels over to the kiva fireplace and tossed them into the fire Blaine had started.

Maria watched this whole procedure without saying a word. She seemed catatonic. Expressionless.

Fernando sat down at the desk to rest for a few minutes while Blaine burned the trash. "Are you okay?" he asked Maria.

Without moving she said, "They will kill me."

"Who will kill you?" Fernando asked.

Maria shrugged. "Jerry. He's still at the house. He's the worst one. He rape me last night."

"Don't worry, we'll take care of Jerry," Fernando said. "We need to get your money for Ricardo's paintings and then send you back to Mexico."

Maria did not respond.

It took Blaine over thirty minutes to burn and dispose the refuse, and then another fifteen minutes to wash the fire pit and burn a stack of newspapers. When he finished, he sat down with Fernando and Maria.

"What now?" Blaine asked, sweat pouring from his forehead.

"You need to pay Maria for the Ricardo paintings you've sold so far," Fernando said. "She'll need cash. Going forward you can do a bank transfer for the paintings you sell. The two of you need to exchange bank information."

Blaine groaned. "Well, fuck. Okay, I guess I can do that. I've sold five paintings so far for a total of fifty thousand dollars. Her eighty percent would come to forty thousand. I'll have to go to the bank and withdraw the money."

"We'll wait right here," Fernando said, turning to Blaine and staring at him until the big man got up to go.

Blaine sighed. "Okay, I'll be right back."

Fernando stopped him. "Wait, let's take care of the body first. The streets will just get more crowded as the day goes on."

The two of them carried the rug and its contents out to the red Toyota. They had to set the rug down while Fernando opened the doors with the keys he'd taken from Diego's pocket. Fernando maneuvered one of the split rear seats down flat to make room for the bulky rug. Then they loaded the body into the back of the vehicle.

With that, Blaine hurried off to the bank while Fernando went back inside the gallery and locked the door behind him.

While they waited for Blaine to return, Fernando considered his options for how to deal with Jerry back at the safe house. All of the options had risks, big risks.

33

Fernando explained his plan, with some attention to contingencies should the plan go awry, as it usually did. Maria and Blaine knew their roles. Discussion finished, they locked up the gallery and climbed into the red Toyota containing Diego's body in the rear compartment. Blaine had to squeeze into the free back seat, snuggled up against the rug. Maria sat in the front passenger seat, as she would if Diego had been driving. Fernando drove. He slumped down in the seat so as to be about the same size as Diego. Seen from a distance, Jerry wouldn't know the difference until it was too late. That, at least, was the plan.

"This is creeping me out," Blaine complained, trying to push the rug further away from him.

"Hold tight. We'll be there in a few minutes," Fernando said.

They drove around the Paseo to Agua Fria and headed west. From a distance they could see Maria's VW camper van parked in front of the safe house. Fernando slowed down as they approached the house.

According to plan, Fernando pulled over about fifty yards away and dropped off Blaine. Cursing, Blaine scrambled out of the rear seat carrying his Glock. Blaine's job was to enter the house through the back door and surprise Jerry from behind as he went out to greet Diego and found Fernando instead. If the door was locked, Blaine would have to pick the lock with the lock pick that Fernando gave him and showed him how to use. One way or another, Blaine had to gain entry and confront Diego from behind.

Fernando and Maria waited in the parked red Toyota and watched Blaine's progress. It was essential to give Blaine enough time to reach the back patio.

When Blaine stepped on the patio, Fernando took off. He drove to the safe house and pulled in behind Maria's VW camper van. Maria jumped out as soon as the red Toyota came to a stop and walked toward the front door of the safe house, as instructed. Her job was to distract Jerry.

When the front door of the safe house opened, Jerry stepped out expecting Diego and Maria in the red Toyota. Maria greeted Jerry and walked toward him. Jerry nodded.

So far, so good.

Just then Fernando heard Blaine cursing and then kicking on the rear door, after failing to get it open with the lock pick. Already the plan had exploded, thanks to Blaine.

Jerry heard the pounding too. He looked wildly around him, spotting Fernando in the driver's seat of the red Toyota. He tried to grab Maria by the arm, but she screamed and managed to free herself from his grasp and then ran behind the VW camper van.

Blaine came running around the corner of the house, waving his Glock in front of him like a crazy man.

Seeing Blaine, Jerry pulled a pistol out of his shoulder holster and fired off a shot at Fernando. The windshield of the red Toyota shattered.

Fernando jumped outside the red Toyota using its driver's side door as cover. He fired one shot a split second before Blaine fired at Jerry.

The two bullets staggered Jerry. He yelped and grabbed his chest. His legs crumbled under him and he fell to his knees and then toppled over face first in the dirt yard.

Maria peeked out from behind the VW camper van.

"I couldn't get inside," Blaine said, seeming to blame Fernando. "I know the plan was for me to come through the house and clobber him from behind, but I couldn't get the fucking lock pick to work. I couldn't get in."

"I heard. Stop complaining," Fernando said. "Help me get him inside before someone sees us."

"Is he still alive?" Blaine asked.

Fernando bent over Jerry and felt for a pulse. "No. There's no pulse. Grab his other arm."

Wearing latex gloves, the two of them dragged Jerry into the house. They sat him slumped back on one of the two sagging sofas. Fernando placed the dead man's gun on the floor in front of the sofa.

"Okay, now follow me," Fernando said, going back outside.

Blaine followed Fernando to the rear of the red Toyota.

Fernando opened the hatch and pulled the rug halfway out of the vehicle. He grabbed one end and told Blaine to take the other. They lugged the heavy rug wrapped around Diego's corpse inside the house and sat it down between the two sofas.

Fernando rested for a moment, trying to catch his breath. Then he took a clean pair of latex gloves out of his back pocket and put them on. Next he unrolled the rug, leaving Diego lying on his back, arms splayed, feet toward the door.

While Blaine watched, Fernando took Diego's pistol and fired off two shots into the wall near the front door. He placed the smoking pistol next to Diego's right hand.

"I want him and the gun positioned like this," Fernando said. "So it looks like the place was raided by a local gang or a bunch of druggies. Like the two of them died in a shoot out. Understand?"

Blaine nodded. "You think the police will buy that?"

"Hah! Are you kidding? The cartel won't go to the police," Fernando said. "They'd have to be crazy. They'd all be locked up. No, the cartel does its own policing. Their way."

"Great," Blaine said. "Why are the fuckers in Santa Fe any way? It's a small town."

"Money," Fernando said. "Lotta people with money in Santa Fe. Where there's people with money, there's people who want to buy drugs."

Before leaving Fernando went into the bedroom and grabbed Maria's suitcase on the floor by the bed. He stuffed in some dirty clothes on the bed and zipped the suitcase closed.

With that, Fernando and Blaine walked out of the house. They left the front door unlocked. Fernando opened a packet of wet wipes and wiped the doorknob clean and then went around back and did the same on the other door. Next he went to the red Toyota and wiped every surface he or the others had touched. Finally he walked back into the house, wiped off the keys to the red Toyota, and put them back in Diego's pocket. Then he joined Blaine and Maria outside.

After watching Fernando wipe off fingerprints, Blaine asked, "I thought you said the police wouldn't be called?"

"They won't," Fernando said. "This is just in case some detective gets curious and decides to do a little freelance work."

Maria was sitting in the driver's seat of the VW camper van. She hadn't said a word since the shooting.

Fernando carried the suitcase to Maria. "You want me to put it in the rear compartment?"

She nodded.

Fernando deposited the suitcase in back and slammed the hatch closed. Then he joined her in the van, sitting in the front passenger seat. They waited for Blaine, who climbed in back.

"Okay, we're done here," Fernando said. "Just take us back to Blaine's gallery and you're free to leave. You have all your belongings, you have money in your pocket, and you should have at least six to eight hours to get a head start. Maybe a lot more if Silva and his boys don't get around to coming over until tomorrow."

Maria listened but said nothing.

"You'll be across the border before nightfall," Fernando continued. "You can stop in Juarez or you can keep going south. Another four hours will get you to Chihuahua."

Still Maria didn't speak. She started the van, put it in gear, and drove carefully out of the drive onto Agua Fria Street. None of them said a word.

When they reached the parking lot at Blaine's gallery, Maria turned off the engine and stepped out of the van. Fernando did the same. She came over to him and threw her arms around his neck and hugged him tightly for several seconds.

Then Maria let go of Fernando and, without saying a word, climbed back in the camper van and drove off, on her way to Mexico.

33

Next afternoon Fidel called Fernando and asked to talk, so they agreed to meet for Happy Hour at El Farol. When five o'clock came around, Fernando walked down Canyon Road to El Farol. He ignored the old codgers sitting on the porch and stepped inside. He was surprised to see Fidel sitting at the bar in front, not at a table in back. Then he saw why. Ruby and her artistic entourage were gathered around the largest table, arguing loudly while passing around pitchers of beer. Their daily merriment was well under way and there would be no opportunity for a serious conversation. In addition to Ruby, he saw Blaine, Wayne, Dave, and a young woman covered with tattoos who looked like a walking advertisement for a tattoo parlor. All that was missing was the name of the parlor on her forehead.

Ruby gave Fernando the finger when she saw him walk in. He waved back. Good old Ruby. You never knew what you did to piss her off.

"Hey, Fernando," Fidel said. He motioned toward the back room. "I wanted to avoid that."

Fernando laughed. "Good choice." He sat on the bar stool next to Fidel, noticing that Fidel wasn't wearing his paisley tie or corduroy jacket today. In fact, he looked a bit bedraggled for the usually dapper reporter, the *Independent's* finest. "So Fidel, what's up?"

Before Fidel could answer, bartender Brad came over and asked, "What can I get you, Fernando? Your usual Modelo draft?"

"Yes indeed," Fernando said. He noticed Fidel was drinking a Corona out of the bottle.

"I just came from a fire out on Agua Fria," Fidel said. "A neighbor reported the fire this morning, according to the firefighters I interviewed. Total loss. They found two badly burned bodies inside. Incinerated beyond recognition. Looks to me like the work of the Sinaloa Cartel. Forensics said it would be difficult, if not impossible, to find a different cause of death, if it wasn't the smoke or the fire that killed them."

Fernando bit his tongue.

"A vehicle in front of the house also burned," Fidel said. "Some sort of Toyota SUV."

"Yeah?" Fernando said.

Fidel nodded. "Here's the thing. The neighbors said a couple of drug dealers were renting the house. Now I know you've had several run-ins with the cartel lately, so I'm wondering. What do you know about this fire and the two dead bodies that may or may not have died in the fire?"

Fernando smiled. It was hard to get anything by Fidel. He was as sharp as they came, from years of being an investigative reporter.

"I'm listening," Fidel said.

"Nothing. I don't know anything about the fire or the bodies," Fernando lied.

Fidel stared at Fernando, skeptical.

"Sorry I can't help you," Fernando said.

Fidel sighed. "Okay, let me know if you change your mind. I have to turn in something for tomorrow's paper. My deadline's in about an hour, so I'm gonna have to leave."

With that, Fidel left a ten-dollar bill on the bar and walked out of El Farol.

Fernando grabbed his Modelo draft and walked back to the table where Ruby and the others were talking loudly. "Mind if I join you?"

"About time you got social," Ruby shot back. "You've been a hermit lately. A morose hermit."

"Nah, just busy," Fernando said, sitting down next to the young woman with tattoos.

"Have you seen Claude?" Wayne asked. "I'm supposed to meet her here."

"Oh, for Christ's sake, Wayne," Ruby said. "Claude's been dead for forty years. Get over it!"

Wayne turned to Ruby. "What? I'm not dead."

Ruby rolled her eyes and shook her head sadly. "I give up."

The young woman tried to make peace. She turned to Fernando. "Yeah, Wayne was just telling us about seeing the Devil on Canyon Road. I believe it, man. I think it's groovy that Wayne can see the Devil. Most people can't, you know. I mean, they're so shallow, they only believe what they can touch and see on this plane. Me, I believe in the Devil, ghosts, witches, you name it. Ghosts especially. I see them all the time on Canyon

Road. They won't hurt you."

"Don't be ridiculous," Ruby said. "What do you mean 'on this plane'?"

"Sure," the tattooed woman said. "We live in a metaverse, not a universe. There are all these planes of existence, maybe millions of them, I don't know. Everything you can dream or imagine exists somewhere, on one of these planes. They have to, or you wouldn't be able to dream or imagine them. You see?"

"You saw Claude?" Wayne interjected.

"No, but I'm sure she's right there on one of the planes. Dead people exist too, you know."

At that Blaine picked up the nearest pitcher and poured more beer into everyone's glass. "Yeah, well, I don't know about the fucking metaverse, but I just saw the Devil too. It doesn't have to be the Devil himself, just his representative. But yeah, I've seen the Devil. He's here. Right now. In Santa Fe."

"Groovy," the tattooed woman said. "I like you," she said to Blaine.

Ruby about choked on her beer. "What about you, Fernando? Have you seen the Devil lately...walking or maybe riding his bicycle on Canyon Road?"

Fernando laughed. "That depends on how you define the Devil, like Blaine says."

"Or what plane you're on," the tattooed woman added.

"Exactly," Fernando said. "If you're talking about the Biblical version—or plane, if that's what you want to call it—then no, I haven't seen him. But if you're talking about someone or something that's pure evil...you get where I'm going with this?"

"Right on, motherfucker!" Blaine blurted out, his eyes wild with excitement and his long black hair shimmering in the late afternoon light coming through the windows of El Farol. He looked unhinged. "Think about this: a name, five letters, beginning with S. Oh, the fucking synchronicity of it, don't you see. Satan and Silva. What does it mean? You tell me!"

"The planes," added the young woman.

"Of course!" Blaine said. "Different planes, different manifestations."

"See, that's what I'm talking about," the young woman said. "He nailed it. Groovy."

Ruby turned to the young woman. "Honey, I haven't heard anyone use that term for twenty years. You might want to re-think your vocabulary."

"Don't be so myopic," the young woman snapped.

At that point Fernando decided he needed to intervene. Ruby was not one to be trifled with. He turned to the young woman and held out his hand. "Fernando Lopez."

The young woman smiled. "Heather Hall."

Fernando's intervention worked, because Ruby turned back to arguing with Blaine.

Wayne just sat in his chair with glazed eyes waiting for Claude. Dave sat next to Wayne, wide-eyed and mute.

Fernando finished his second beer and decided he better leave before Blaine could pour him another glass. Blaine could drink all night. Fernando couldn't.

He excused himself and stood up to go. Ruby nodded but no one else even noticed.

Fernando walked out of El Farol and saluted the old codgers who were still sitting on the patio. He started walking the short distance up Canyon Road to his office. He'd lost track of the time. He wondered if Fidel had filed his story yet and what he had written about the fire and the two bodies. He guessed he would find out tomorrow morning when he read the *Independent*.

One block up he saw a black Range Rover coming toward him on Canyon Road. He recognized the car as soon as he saw the darkened windows. The car slowed to a stop in the middle of the street, a good twenty feet from where Fernando was walking.

Fernando's first impulse was to run. His second impulse was to reach for his Smith & Wessen. Unfortunately, he'd left his gun at the office, since he was only going out to meet Fidel at El Farol, a couple blocks away. How dangerous could that be? He was about to find out.

While Fernando stood frozen, the proverbial deer caught in headlights, the left rear window of the Range Rover buzzed down and Silva Archivada's face glared at him from the shadows inside the Range Rover. It was like an old time black and white horror movie, the scene where the monster appears. Silva slowly extended his right hand through the open window, with his thumb straight up and his trigger finger pointing at Fernando. Then Silva quickly snapped back his trigger finger and said, "Bang!"

Instantly the window buzzed up and the black Range Rover with darkened windows drove off.

Fernando stood on the side of the street and watched the Range Rover disappear down Canyon Road.

READERS GUIDE

1. Why do some people believe the Devil has appeared on Canyon Road? How reliable is Wayne Fontenot, who first reported this sighting to Private Investigator Fernando Lopez?

2. How does the murder of the homeless person under the Delgado Street Bridge support the belief that a Devil has appeared on Canyon Road. Or does it?

3. Explain the 'Take Back our Streets' political movement led by Rodger Barkley and Homer Tryzinski, both of whom are running for Santa Fe City Council. How does Lopez feel about the movement? Why?

4. How and what does Lopez learn about Ricardo Aragon, a painter from L.A. living with his wife Maria and brother Oscar in an abandoned A-frame near Wayne Fontenot?

5. Why does Lopez pay a visit to the A-frame rented by the Aragons? What does he find there? Who are the Aragons?

6. Lopez discovers that one of the men who attacked a homeless camp at Fort Marcy Park works at Homer's Diner, owned by City Council candidate Homer Tryzinski, a leader of the 'Take Back Our Streets' movement. Later, when another homeless man is murdered, Santa Fe Police raid Homer's Diner. What do they find at the diner? Why do Tryzinski and Barkley end their campaigns for City Council?

7. When Blaine Rogers hosts a reception at his gallery for Ricardo Aragon, Lopez discovers that Aragon is a "blood painter." What is a blood painter? How does this development help Lopez make sense of recent events in Santa Fe?

8. During Blaine's reception for Ricardo Aragon, Lopez once again investigates the A-frame where the Aragons live and encounters someone--or something--humming outside the A-frame. Later Maria comes to Lopez's office to ask for help. What does Maria tell Lopez about Ricardo's brother, Oscar. What does Lopez about why they have come to Santa Fe?

9. Why is the Sinaloa Cartel after the Aragon family? Who is Silva Archivada?

10. When Santa Fe Police find Oscar Aragon's body hanging from the Delgado Street Bridge, what mystery does it clear up?

11. Both Lopez and Santa Fe Police Detective Manny Alvarez attempt to protect the Aragons when the Aragons are attacked by Sinaloa gunmen at the A-frame. What are the results? What happens to Maria?

12. How do the Santa Fe Police track down the Sinaloa safe house where the gunmen are staying? What else do they discover at the house?

13. Why does Silva Archivada visit Lopez? What does he want?

14. How and where does Lopez finally find Maria? How do Lopez and Blaine help Maria escape from the Sinaloa Cartel?

15. Lopez and Archivada confront each other at the very end of the story. What are the implications for the future?